Riding a Tiger

The self-criticism of Arnold Fisher

Riding a Tiger
The self-criticism of Arnold Fisher

Robert Abel

Asia 2000 Limited
Hong Kong

© 1998 Robert Abel
All rights reserved

ISBN 962-7160-50-4

Published by Asia 2000 Ltd
1101 Seabird House,
22–28 Wyndham Street, Central,
Hong Kong

http://www.asia2000.com.hk/

Typeset with Ventura Publisher in Adobe Garamond by Asia 2000
Printed in Hong Kong by Regal Printing

First printing 1998

This book is wholly a work of fiction and no reference is intended in it to any real person, living or dead. Some places and institutions are real, but any people associated with them are imagined. This book is sold subject to the condition that it shall not, by way of trade or otherwise, be lent, resold, hired out or otherwise circulated without the publisher's prior written consent in any form of binding or cover other than that in which it is published and without a similar condition including this condition being imposed on the subsequent purchaser.

To my Chinese friends

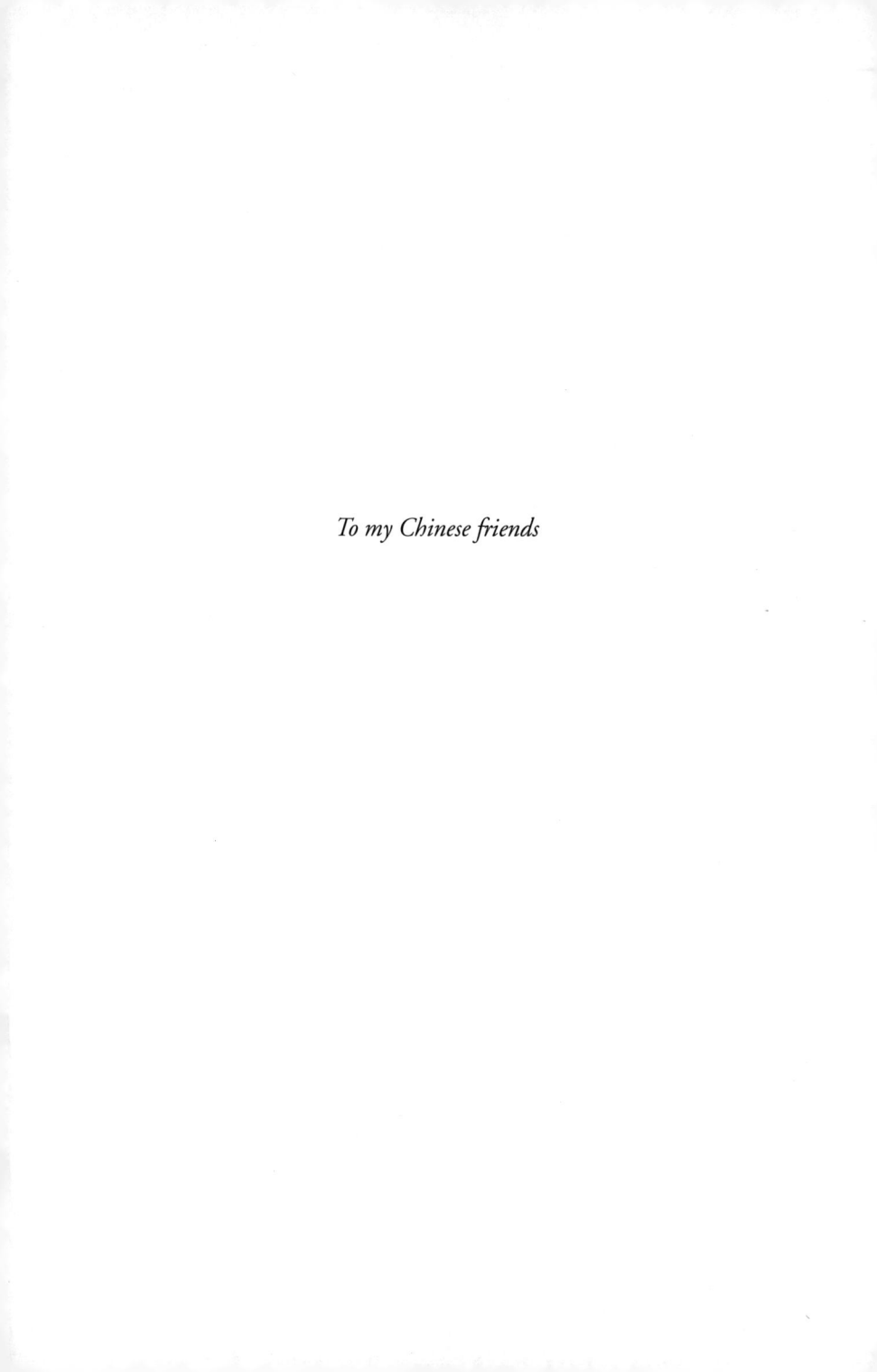

Introduction

COMRADES: the document which follows is the testimony of Arnold Fisher, a citizen of the United States of America who was brought to the People's Republic of China eighteen months ago as a foreign expert. He was assigned to the programming work unit in The China Electrical Engineering Company, Beijing. The self-criticism was called for after allegations about Mr. Fisher's immoral conduct were brought forward by Wu Ko-chu, a student at Beijing University. In subsequent investigations, sufficient reason was found to detain Mr. Fisher not only on grounds of immoral conduct, but crimes against the state as well. Indeed, further charges may be filed.

He is not a spy, but apparently a trafficker in illegal goods and a man of decadent standards of conduct.

Because of the delicate nature of the People's Republic's relationship to America at the present time, Mr. Fisher was placed under house arrest at You Yi Bing Guan (the Friendship Hotel) and asked to supply this self-criticism. We had hoped that the self-examination would lead him to political re-evaluation of his conduct and a confession of his crimes so that his punishment would not complicate exchange programs and relationships with his country. His cooperation can be rated as inconsistent at best, however, and much of the testimony contained herein was obtained only by interrogation. In the main, the confession was composed in the privacy of his rooms; but portions were also added by our stenographer when we found it necessary to question Mr. Fisher's interpretation of events, or simply to spur him on with his narrative. Therefore, it is not an orderly proceeding and our committees are still evaluating Mr. Fisher's conclusions for evidence of rehabilitation.

The American Embassy has taken only passing interest in this case as yet, but it is not always easy to make staff of that agency believe that conduct like that of Mr. Fisher may have dire consequences. Mr. Fisher himself seems often to be unaware of, or even to flaunt, the fact that his crimes may be capital. Therefore, given the international implications, and the possible severity of the result, we ask the members of the reviewing committees to give the following document their most careful and considered attention.

[Signed] *Zhang Zhang-ho*, chief of protocol and political theory, northeast bureau, Chinese Communist Party. 8/10/88.

(The Party seal, containing a large red star, is here affixed.)

Comrades!

You have not given me enough paper.

Last night as I lay here in what I know to be the utter, probably decadent luxury of my hotel room, I realized that if I am to explain myself to you, per your demands, I must begin at the beginning. And the beginning goes a long way back.

Worse, I have had a vision of how interconnected are the fates and actions of every one of us. This vision has staggered me into incoherence.

But I am going to be frank, comrades, in what you may feel is that offensive Yankee way. The devils are in the details and I intend to worry those devils until I am satisfied that my own truth has been revealed. My truth. My portion of the whole truth. My sentence in the paragraph, my chapter in the novel, my place in the chorus line.

It's a damned nuisance, and no one wants to get this over with more quickly than me. Therefore: more paper, please.

Comrades!

I think you have misunderstood my request. Two more sheets of paper added to the fifteen you already gave me is only seventeen pages total. Comrade Sun has explained that to procure more paper will require — this is not my fault! — paperwork. But truly, comrades, as I am under threat of death, I believe that seventeen pages is unconscionably few for a self-defense, confession, and rehabilitation that will persuade all parties concerned that I have realized the magnitude of my crimes and now have a politically correct perspective.

Understanding how tiresome paperwork is (believe me!), and understanding also that execution — *why* do I use that word? — of my request for more paper might delay proceedings that we all desire speedily culminated, please allow me to make a suggestion or two. To wit:

I have a friend at Foreign Languages Press who has supplied quantities of scrap paper (misprinted or waste paper, or sheets cut out of square — good-quality bond) in the past. May I contact her? This would be off the record, of course.

I have also in the past been able to procure writing paper from the Telefax operators in Building N° 1 here. They were kind enough to supply me on occasion with the extra paper, scrap paper, discarded carbon copies and botched photocopy pages in their wastebaskets at the end of a working day. Foreign journalists and businessmen frequently leave these materials behind, oblivious to their value in a tree-scarce, hence paper-

Riding a Tiger

scarce country. Did they never ask the reasons for all the reforestation in progress? I can use the unused side of these pages.

I hope mentioning these facts will in no way incriminate or bring difficulty to people who showed me considerable kindness in the face of the ongoing paper shortage.

Comrades!

I am shocked and dismayed at your complaints that I am attempting to prolong the completion of my self-criticism in a ploy to prolong also my miserable life, to avoid judgment, by demanding more paper. I appeal to your sense of proportion:

my life: seventeen pieces of paper.

Is this just?

I refuse to participate in a charade, and since the purpose of this self-criticism is to explore the truth of how crimes against the state and against our fellow citizens are initiated, then I must insist on giving a full accounting. As a foreigner especially, I believe I have to articulate the psychology, the ecology, if you will, of my decisions, step by step, and supply every detail, up to and beyond the moment when Chen Tai-pan was killed.

We believe he was murdered, comrade Fisher.

Murdered, whatever.

Seventeen pages is insufficient for this!

PS. Another place I have found paper is this: *The China Daily* is sometimes delivered to the hotel in bundles that are wrapped with blank signatures of newsprint. One of these blank signatures is worth about 32 typewriter pages, if I write on both sides. Perhaps Comrade Sun would be kind enough to meet the *China Daily* delivery man and secure five or six of these signatures in good condition — no rips, smears, footprints, no rain puckers. The creative process requires good quality paper. This *is* important!

Comrades!

My sincere thanks for the ample supply of Beijing Friendship Hotel air mail stationery which you supplied me with this morning. I appreciate the time taken to collect these pads and the sacrifice this will entail for residents here, many of them foreign experts like myself who might be expected to feel keenly the loss of this kind of communication to their friends and loved ones. I believe that I now have twenty-one tablets averaging seventeen pages each, or 357 pages total (714 counting both sides), far more than I anticipate using to tell my story.

    PS. I especially enjoyed the spicy tofu dish Mr. Sun brought last night. In the future, may I ask for Beijing Beer instead of Wu Sying (Five Star)? This may seem a quibble, but I'm sure my self-criticism will touch on why this is an important request. I realize I already enjoy considerable amenities for a criminal of my stripe, and I don't expect to be coddled. I intend to cooperate fully, and not just because my life depends on it! Attention to these details, meanwhile, will expedite the completion of my task.

    It's so complicated! Even a hat, a "mere" hat has significance.

    PPS. Special thanks to Mr. Sun for allowing me to plug in my voltage adapter so that I can use tape recorder and humidifier.

    PPPS. Is it too much to ask that the guards move their ping-pong table down the hall a ways? Trying to compose a decent sentence with all that *ka-tick ka-tock* is next to impossible.

Mr. Fisher, you have written nothing for us for 24 hours. Please explain yourself.

    I don't know where to begin. I start here, there. Then it all gets confused.

You mentioned a hat. You said a "mere hat" was important.

    Is it politically correct to begin with a hat?

It will not be convenient to feed you until you begin.

    I think I can begin now.

I

COMRADES:

I was bicycling down Chang An Avenue one morning in June and having a hell of a time of it because of the wind. My mouth and nose were covered by a surgeon's mask, the kind you Chinese wear all winter and during the spring when the winds carry that salmon-pink dust from the northern deserts and slap it in your face and eyes and sandpaper all the exposed skin in Beijing. The dust was wicked on this hot, dry day, and one gust not only slammed me practically to a halt, but ripped my hat off and sent it sailing down the street behind me.

Of course I couldn't *see* the hat tumbling down the street, but its trajectory was readily imaginable. To anyone but a native, comrades, it would be a little difficult to explain why such a merely irritating event in most cases was a very, very irritating event in Beijing. In the first place, as you know, Chang An is a very wide thoroughfare, as most roads are which course through political officialdom (on the Madrid model, we could say — allowing a clear line of fire and making it difficult also for anyone to erect a quick blockade — can we say this?) and the outermost traffic lanes reserved for bicycles are thronged at the hour I was, like about nine million others, pedaling to work. Such a river of cyclists requires certain etiquette to prevent a mass tangling of bicycles and people. No way could I just jam on the brakes, turn around, and retrieve my hat. Easier to swim up Niagara Falls. I had instead to make my way to the curb, dismount, stand my bike and run back along the sidewalk in hopes of spying my hat and then finding enough of an opening in the river of wheels to grab it without getting crushed.

What, you are asking yourselves, could make a hat, a silly hat, so important to me? Please understand, comrades, although I was in the prime of life (a mere forty-five), my hair had taken a permanent vacation some years hence. Beijing, so cold in winter, is nevertheless on the same latitude as our Washington, DC — one could make too much of this coincidence — and the sun can be merciless. Without a hat, I suffered terrible headaches after only a few hours in the China sun, and to me it was an instrument of survival — not of identity, as some of the hotel barflies insisted. I couldn't just let the hat blow away.

Besides that, the hat had been given to me by a Chinese woman of intense interest to me, and I couldn't imagine saying to her "Oh, it blew away somewhere along Chang An." You are not in any case so cavalier about goods in China and you understand very well, I think, the special value of goods given in friendship. The hat was English, a golf-style cap, and it probably set Cao Song-wen back half a week's pay.

But what, Mr. Fisher, were you, an American foreign expert, one receiving such vast remuneration (almost ten times that of your Chinese colleagues), doing on a bicycle when the work unit provided a taxi daily, for the express purpose of chauffeuring you to and from work?

Yes, I understand your pique, but I was not looking a gift horse in the mouth, as we say. God knows how that phrase will translate. For the time being, I hope you will be satisfied with a somewhat superficial explanation, but I will get to the root of your concern in due course. I was en-bicycled, thus, because:

1) I needed the exercise. Contrary to expectations, the Chinese diet I had enjoyed for the last year had not stripped off those extra American pounds so unsightly to the Chinese, so symbolic of decadent excesses, and so distressing to me personally, for the usual middle-aged reasons, but made more poignant in my case because of my interest in the woman who had given me the hat.

2) I wanted to experience life as you Chinese live it — endure it, enjoy it, suffer it. Taking to the streets on a bicycle was a way of feeling the pulse a little more authentically, made me understand a little better the privations and stresses of the men and women in my computer seminars.

3) The taxi driver, Wen Da-xing, was using the time assigned to chauffeur me to the office to engage in an enterprise which we conspired in and which was meant to enrich three lives significantly. By this I mean, to be precise, that taxi driver Wen Da-xing and the beautiful hat-giver Cao Song-wen were at that very moment about sixty miles north of Beijing in a dusty little village loading the taxi with watermelons.

You see, comrades, that all of us were at that moment in the grip of capitalist ideas. And it was my capital that the beautiful Cao Song-wen was counting into the hands of the watermelon supplier and which would be the basis for our foray into free-enterprise marketing, greasing the wheels of a few other projects I will confess in due time, and greasing also the palms of a few neighborhood officials.

One question you may not have thought to ask, I suspect, is what part a hat can play in the fate of capitalist and criminal schemes? In the case of my British golfer, the role was not insignificant. Alas, at least indirectly, it was to lead to my undoing!

Riding a Tiger

I saw, as I was dashing against the flow of bicycles along Chang An that morning, that my hat had been blown and propelled to the very outermost edge of the bicycle lane and was, in fact, imperiled by the tires of the busses, trucks and taxis pummeling by. While I was agitatedly waiting for a breach in the flow of bicycles to dash to the hat's rescue, I saw a young woman coast to a halt, reach down, pluck the hat up, and cycle away. I tried shouting to her, but the uproar of traffic and the continuous clangor of the bicycle bells (bells are used instead of brakes in Beijing, to no effect that I have been able to observe) made it a silly exercise.

There were, however, a few things of note about the young woman who had plucked up my cap: she was wearing a very pretty summer skirt, a kind of rosy purple, she had on sunglasses, and — most unusual of all — she was riding a red, woman's style bicycle. Since most Chinese women on their way to work wear dark slacks, since few Chinese can afford sunglasses, and since most Chinese bicycles are big, black or green and unisex, the chances were good, I thought, that this young woman was, in fact, a Chinese-American, possibly even a student or foreign expert like myself.

Confident in this illusion, I gave heroic chase. This obviously is an easy thing for me to say, but comrades I do not overdramatize. You can imagine, I'm sure, that bicycling in rush-hour Beijing for a middle-aged man unaccustomed to pedaling your Hong Chi (Red Spirit) of the twenty-eight inch wheels is no trifling exercise. You will also appreciate that for me it has never been a simple matter to move along faster than the already vigorous but gentlemanly pace of the Beijing bicycle horde, and that there are an incredible number of hazards that present themselves to the cyclist who deems it necessary to rush. Busses, for example, routinely sidle into the bicycle lane to unload and gather passengers, and these custard and burgundy double-length leviathans can not only blast you with exhaust and cyclones of that miserable red dust, but funnel you into a dead end where your only choice is to stop and wait for the bus passengers to clear, or ram into them — an alternative not as despised as one would hope. The bicycle lane is also chock-a-block with huge tricycles carrying everything from bamboo brooms in bundles resembling shocks of corn, to freshly butchered swine (I returned the smiles of several), from a beautiful pyramid of cabbages to stinking black barrels full of night soil. And at every intersection waves of bicyclists collide and cross the lanes of automotive traffic and all the rhythm and flow of the commuting pace collapses utterly into self-interested chaos that even the policemen — respected as they are — cannot whistle or wave or command into order. Similar jam-ups await us at every roadside free-market, too. To be in a hurry, therefore, is to — pardon the expression — challenge the gods.

I must also acknowledge that the young woman who scooped up my hat was obviously used to cycling, and although she seemed to be pedaling quite gracefully and easily, she was, in truth, setting a hell of a pace for a fat foreign devil like me. I was feeling strain where I never felt strain before — for example, in that little indentation in one's hip, where the thigh bones join the pelvis. (And what I was feeling that morning as I pummeled along in so ardent pursuit of my cap I would feel again two days later in double measure.)

Finally, however, I pulled athwart the lass — who had insouciantly donned my golfer now, and looked pretty pert in it, too, I confess. The hat fitted her thanks only to a superabundance of the black hair she sported, for her face was otherwise small, round, and composed as a ceramic plate. The wind was still coming at us, hard, and had driven the skirt above her knees and pressed her blouse tightly against her body so that it was instantly apparent that this was a vigorous and unusually attractive young lady.

Then as now, I knew very little Chinese, but at least enough so that when I had startled her into realizing I meant to speak to her, even ripping along as we were, to say "that is mine" as I pointed to the hat on her head. She regarded me as if I had said something quite comic and smiled in a way I can only describe as "merry", old-fashioned as that will sound, but shook her head, "no," and declared in Chinglish, with a wonderful upward lilt and emphasis on the second word: "Is *not* your hat."

I tried to mimic what had happened because I could not remember the word for "wind" (*feng* or *feng li* as I now know) and I can only guess what the woman made of my gestures and gyrations for she began to laugh so hard she nearly lost control of her bicycle. When she regained composure, she pointed to a traffic island and shouted "Stop there!" I coasted behind her, narrowly missed clipping the rear fender of her bicycle and found myself almost embarrassingly close when I managed to rein in my old China cruiser.

"Do you speak English?" I asked.
"Such a little bit."
"You see, what happened is this. . . ."
"I know, I know," she said, removing the hat. "The wint."
"Yes, the wind."

"The wind blow down your hat."

"That's right."

"Maybe you are *duwanjier?* Foreign expert?"

"Yes. I work for China Electronics Engineering." I said the name in Chinese. "A teacher."

"Oh yes? I work very near."

"Where? The name?"

"I don't know English." She gave the Chinese name of her work unit, a clerical office in a petroleum products factory.

"I don't know much Chinese, either," I said.

"Too bad," the girl said, with an easy smile.

"Thank you for returning my hat."

"Welcome." She took off her sunglasses and tilted her head to get a good look at me, rather like looking at a painting or some odd, unfamiliar object. I had been in China just long enough to be used to this unabashed staring you Chinese sometimes seem to enjoy. "What do you call this?" She cupped her chin in her hand.

"A beard."

"Beard," she repeated. "Is marvelous thing!"

I laughed, a bit embarrassed. "Thank you." Bicycles were streaming past, bells jangling. "Where do you study English?"

"Books only. Television."

"On your own?"

She shrugged. "I don't know this meaning."

"By yourself. No teacher."

"No teacher. Yes. I like to have teacher, but no luck."

"I'll be your teacher," I said.

"No!" she said in disbelief. "I cannot pay."

"You teach me Chinese, I teach you English." I pulled out my wallet and gave her my card. Then I said in Chinese that I lived at the Friendship Hotel (You Yi Bing Guan) and that I would like to practice Chinese with her once or twice a week.

"And I can study English?"

"Sure. Why not?"

She put the card in the pocket of her skirt where it didn't look very secure to me. I felt a little silly suddenly, old foreign fart talking to this exquisite Chinese youth. She patted her thigh, her wonderfully solid thigh, mounted her bicycle, and said,

"Maybe."

"I hope so," I said. "What is your name?"

She laughed lightly, donned her sunglasses and pushed into the traffic. I followed her for a few blocks and she did look back once or twice, and she did smile. When she turned south on Xie Dan Jie, I waved and was damned certain I was seeing the last of her. Too bad! I thought. What a sweet girl.
    Comrades! What can I say? Surely it was at this moment that the first watermelons were being loaded into the Nº 1 taxi of China Electronics Engineering Company. I retied my surgical mask, pulled my hat to my eyebrows, and cycled on.

2

So far you have mentioned *these facts about Cao Song-wen: she gave you a hat, she was paying for watermelons with your money, and you were "interested" in her. Please tell us about your relationship with Ms. Cao.*

I met Ms. Cao in the course of business at China Electronics. She had studied in America for two years, was the unit's premier programmer, and an apparent leader in the whole enterprise. Even her bosses came to her for advice.

Bosses is a capitalist term. We have only unit leaders, Danwei.

She used the term "bosses" and that's why I used it, too. I'm sure she only meant to phrase things in a way that an American would understand.

In any case, it evolved that our relationship was quite complex. Because she spoke English so well, she was often assigned to look after me, or to help me through the bureaucratic maze, to translate my ideas and the information I brought for her colleagues, and even to help me mail things at the post office, or shop for gifts — all the everyday things that become so staggeringly difficult when you cannot even read the signs to the laundry room or speak the language. I'm afraid I became quite dependent on her. She was my right arm.

This was a role she did not assume gladly. She was, I think, delighted to be able to speak English with an American. On the other hand, I was obviously an added burden, took time away from her own private affairs and increased her workload.

There was another important element to all this. I think that at first she was quite jealous and resentful of me. After all, she had studied diligently in America for two years, and had returned to become the resident expert in her unit. She was the center of a lot of attention and respect. When I appeared it was assumed — and not always correctly — that I would have the latest technological word, that I was the new star in the band.

As a novice in the system, I also was naive about the care with which Ms. Cao had set up operations and simply the way she had laid out certain procedures — with an eye also to many things I couldn't appreciate, such as the personalities and needs of the many workers involved. What I saw was a lot of duplication and some old-fashioned programming techniques, general inefficiency as an American businessman would see it. I expressed myself bluntly, American-style, without due regard for Ms.

Cao's position and feelings, without any sense at all of the — what name should I give it? — *chi,* or *esprit* of the work unit itself. In America we sometimes use the expression "Bull in a china shop", a phrase without the ironies of the present context. That was me, almost literally. And here was Ms. Cao translating ideas and remarks from me that were embarrassing to her, even insulting, and subversive of her own authority.

Comrades! What were her choices in this situation?

a) She could have translated dutifully and resented every minute of it, and in the process come to hate me; b) she could say anything she liked and pretend it was translation, and grow to think of me as quite stupid and pathetic; or c) she might patiently try to explain to me the complexities and realities of her situation and hope I would understand and make adjustments, at least speak more appreciatively of her way of doing things.

What did Ms. Cao, being human, and being Chinese, do? She did all three in approximately the order described, a process that coincided with my own ability to realize and understand — and want to correct — the disruptions and chaos I was creating. If she had immediately come to me with pleas and warnings about her role in the work unit and the delicate interplay of personalities involved, I would have assumed at once that I was being hustled to serve her interests and increase her local power. It was only when I began to perceive that my lordly prescriptions were *not working,* had endured some frustration over "the stupid Chinese", had looked around for someone like Ms. Cao to blame for subverting my wisdom, then turned on myself as a poor teacher who knew next to nothing about his students, that I became ripe for understanding Ms. Cao's position and, beyond that, her unique ability to help me teach and do the job I had been hired to do.

I'm not sure when it was we began to talk seriously to each other about what was going on. But I am sure it was very nearly simultaneous with more personal revelations, more intimate confessions that passed between us, originating no doubt in the weariness of an extra-long and trying day, or in the expression of special gratitude for some special service done as though it were an ordinary thing.

For of course Ms. Cao, in her dutiful relation to me, in her official capacity, could have assumed, justifiably, the role of the worker martyring herself on the cutting stone of international relations for the sake of the four modernizations. She could have made it clear, as many Chinese in service assignments love to do, that she was leaving a trail of blood behind for every action she undertook on my behalf. But there was never a whiff of that from her. She was just too damned tough!

It seems to me that many of you Chinese have a sentimental strain (as many Americans do, myself included), and this is not necessarily a condemnation. I think it is one reason why US Country-Western music is so popular in the People's Republic. Ms. Cao liked country music for different reasons: a) she had been to the US and the music reminded her of her time there; b) she regarded it as working class music; and c) she thought it was humorous, and sometimes a little racy, which by Chinese standards it often is. But a sentimentalist Ms. Cao was not, is not, will never be.

This does not mean that she could not be quite sweet and charming, or had no sense of humor. Pragmatic as she was, realistic as she was, she was still a woman capable of deep emotion. Like many people, she was sometimes depressed about events in her own life, or the state of the world. She was also, on the other hand, a ready wit, and could enjoy a kind of teasing, playful repartee that was right next to insulting. I noticed, in time, that she also had quite an active streak of jealousy, and a bit more ambition than most, and hence also a lot of pent-up frustration with the inflexibility of the bureaucracy, the seeming permanence of everything around her. Perhaps her years in America had ruined forever the well-developed patience of most other Chinese. Ms. Cao was eager for change — personal, professional, national.

This requires explanation.
What does?
The changes Ms. Cao was eager for.
Doesn't everyone want change? For the better?
What changes did she want in the nation?
An example, comrades: Ms. Cao was typically a very pragmatic dresser. She wore black or dark blue slacks and heavy sweaters all winter long. She rarely wore a skirt, but when she did it was quite basic. With her little, round glasses and her hair done up in a bun — she had much more hair than met the eye, I was eventually to learn — she could contrive to look almost plain, though in fact I thought from the first she had an animated and attractive face and a sweet, lithe figure, a little on the thin side. She could, in other words, have dressed to dazzle if she so desired. Instead, she dressed in a very humble way, making no effort to draw attention to, or enhance her attractive physical features, which were several.

You found her attractive?

Oh yes! The longer I stayed in China, the more attractive she became. You will recall, meanwhile, that she had been assigned by her work unit to help me get along. We saw a lot of each other every day, six days a week, ten hours or more every day. She kind of grew on me, you see.

But, to return to the topic, there was at the You Yi Bing Guan a kind of United Nations of Barflies, and one day one of the British journalists showed up wearing a bright yellow sweater with this legend emblazoned on it:

HAPPY OUR
COUNTRY,
RICH AND STRONG

The sweatshirt was Chinese-made, but the legend was in English.

Now, comrades, I don't mean to be offensive, but the fact is the sweater was an instant hit among the UNB — United Nations of Barflies — many of them splendid lads and lasses, by the way — don't get me wrong — because it seemed to the members ... well ... *funny*. Not just kitsch exactly, but the *way* the sweater was lettered, making the HAPPY OUR large and noticeable and the other words small and, therefore, less important, as any advertising expert would tell you. And you see, there is in America and England an institution among drinkers and the bars and pubs they frequent called the HAPPY HOUR — usually the first hour after work and the hour before dinner. The idea is that in this one hour after work one has a few drinks and is happy. Presumably work has made them unhappy and returning to their families is an equally grim prospect, and therefore this one hour of boozing is set aside for enjoyment. The point is the UNB members began purchasing the sweaters to celebrate the HAPPY OUR, and the sweater became *de rigeur* as a gift, a common purchase among us, and I ended up with one (courtesy of an otherwise dour Australian teaching at Beijing Foreign Language Institute) which I, for a lark, wore to work.

When Ms. Cao saw this sweater, comrades, she exclaimed:

"That's priceless! Where did you get it?"

I told her.

"How much is it, do you know? Could you get me one?"

"I'll try," I said, "and if I can't get one, I'll let you have this one."

"I wouldn't take your sweater!"

"Why not? Too big?" I patted my belly.

"No. Because it's yours."

"Listen," I said, "all the favors you've done for me, I owe you something."

"But not your shirt."

"Well, not this one, then. But another. What size are you?"

She wrote the numbers down, since she could not expect me to remember the comparatively complex — and varied and accurate — Chinese sizes.

Comrades! I bought Cao Song-wen this HAPPY OUR country sweater, she donned it immediately, and wore it, often, with pride, entirely innocent of the attributes of camp we foreigners had so rudely assigned to it.

What question does this answer?

How Ms. Cao felt about China. Feels. She is very nationalistic. She wants China to be rich and strong.

What personal and professional changes did she desire?

Basically, professionally, she wanted to be able to advance in her career, and to make more money. She told me once, "the incentive I feel is the incentive to rot in place." If she had no revolutionary idealism, comrades, and did not feel that she was indeed serving a greater public and national — and international — interest, even in a minuscule way, she would have given up. But unlike many people in her own work unit, she continued to care.

Naturally, this was related to her personal life. She wanted more money to be able to buy more things. She wanted to work fewer hours to be able to do more, to travel in her own country, to visit old friends and family members. She wanted only what every worker wants: leisure, spending money, freedom to travel, easier family life. More time, more choice.

One day we taxied back from a meeting with a construction brigade that wanted to know if using the computer could help them with a host of problems ranging from correct estimates of materials needed for large-scale projects, to expediting distribution and inventory-taking, to designing, evaluating and redesigning roadways, bridges, rail systems, even airports. It was very late at night and I could see that Ms. Cao was very tired. She was quite unusually subdued, possibly not just from fatigue but also from the prospect of the monumental amount of work entailed in simply answering the construction brigade's inquiries, let alone the actual programming that lay ahead. She had been alert, patient, efficient, tactful all evening, and now there was just this taxi ride between her and well-deserved oblivion.

"I'm sorry to keep you from your family so much," I said. "But I couldn't have done this without you."

She shrugged. "It's my responsibility, too."

"I imagine your husband is a little irritated. I think you see more of me lately than you do of him."

"*Mei guanxi,*" she said, meaning, "it doesn't matter." "When I was in America for two years, we got used to it."

"If I were away from my wife for two years," I said, "I don't know if would *have* a wife when I returned."

"Maybe I don't have a husband." She looked out the window as she spoke. The streets were lit intermittently with a dusty, peach-colored light that now and then glinted on her glasses. The taxi driver (not our regular work unit driver, which might help to account for this unusually personal note from Ms. Cao) was playing a tape of "Western" music, some very sentimental string music that he had apparently been saving up for the moment a Westerner fell into his clutches. The music was quite loud so I had to lean close to Ms. Cao to hear her.

"May I ask why you say that?"

"It's not important," she said, and I assumed the discussion was closed. But a moment later she faced me with unusual candor and asked, "do you miss your wife?"

"I do," I said. "I'm beginning to miss her very much."

"What is she like?"

That was not, of course, an easy question to answer. I said that she was intelligent, hard-working, ambitious, pretty, and that after twenty years we had grown rather used to each other and our habits and tics and needs.

"You are very lucky," Ms. Cao said. "In China, not so many marriages are happy."

"Not all are happy in America, either." I recounted the usual statistics on divorce. "I don't even know that my marriage is *happy*. It's comfortable, agreeable, pleasant."

"You sleep with your wife still?"

I can't tell you how surprised I was by this question. I'm sure you will agree that it is quite unusual for the subject of sex to be broached between Chinese people and foreigners. "Yes."

"Often?"

"Now and then."

"How often?"

"I don't know what to say." I laughed, a little embarrassed. "Once a week?"

Riding a Tiger 23

Ms. Cao nodded, looked away. "My husband has no spirit," she said. "He sleeps on the sofa. He says this is birth control, but I don't think there is much danger of an outburst of passion from him. He does nothing much any more, cares nothing about his work. We never talk about anything much, just hello, good-bye." She looked at me again. "So you see it's not so important that I am not often at home. Sometimes I don't even want to go home. The apartment smells of cigarettes. He leaves his dishes. His beer bottles. But I have nowhere else to go."

"I'm sorry to hear this," I said.

"It doesn't matter. I'm being foolish to mention it."

"It seems such a waste," I said. "Such a beautiful woman, such an unhappy marriage."

"I am not beautiful," she said. "The marriage is bearable."

"Of course you can choose how you want to live," I said. "Surely you could have something better than a 'bearable' marriage?"

"Could I?" Ms. Cao said this in a very acid tone, as if I had insulted her.

"I'm sorry. I didn't mean to sound presumptuous."

"If I divorced, where would I live?" she asked. "I can't go home to my parents. They have one room and a kitchen. I would be assigned to the single women's dormitory, with its communal bath and kitchen. I am thirty-one, too old to marry again. I say this because it is very difficult for a Chinese woman to find a husband after thirty. Beyond this, divorce in China takes a long time."

"Have you given up on your husband? Is there a chance he might change, if you told him how you feel?"

She leaned her forehead into the palm of her hand momentarily, then spoke with disgust. "When I talk to him about how I feel, he becomes ill. He becomes like a baby. I told you, he has no spirit. He has died."

"This is very sad news," I said. "I wish I could help you somehow."

"Don't worry about it," Ms. Cao said. "It's not your problem."

"Of course not," I said. "But I feel concerned for you."

"It's not so unusual," Ms. Cao said. "I can live with it." She leaned forward abruptly and spoke to the taxi driver in clipped, commanding tones. "I told him to stop that awful music. You don't mind?"

"No. Not at all."

When we reached Ms. Cao's apartment building, I couldn't resist touching her on the shoulder as I said good night. She touched my hand in reply, very, very briefly, and said,

"For an American, you're very kind."

I thanked her, but she had already shut the door and was telling the taxi driver where to take me. As soon as he pulled into traffic, he began to play that dreadful sentimental music again. Perverse as it was, comrades, given the dire content of Ms. Cao's confession, I felt quite lifted up, that I had finally had a real conversation with a real adult in China. Consequently, my esteem for Ms. Cao flowered, and I truly did hate to think of such a beautiful, young woman going to waste, and her spirit resigning itself to such a flaccid existence.

Oh, I fantasized, comrades, but never did it occur to me that such a fantasy could be fulfilled!

When did Ms. Cao give you the hat?

Oh, yes, the hat! It was not long after the conversation I just described. I was getting terrible headaches every afternoon, and I knew it was a sinus problem, not one you like to mention to other people, brought on by dry air, dust, and sunburn. Ms. Cao became concerned, however, and pried a complaint from me. One afternoon, the pain was really severe and she insisted on taking me to the unit health clinic.

Go on. What happened there?

Sorry, I'm finding it difficult to concentrate this morning. At the health clinic, nothing happened. I didn't have my blue card. It was in my hotel room, and the officious little bitch at reception refused to admit me without my blue card. She and Ms. Cao had quite a tiff, but I wasn't feeling well enough to endure a bureaucratic battle and returned to the office where I fell into an awful, headachy, nightmare-filled nap right at the desk. Ms. Cao noted when I awoke that it was my good fortune not to be bleeding to death when we went to the clinic because the receptionist seemed to believe that death would be approximately the right punishment for showing up at a health clinic without blue card credentials — or perhaps maiming and then death, followed by corpse mutilation, Ms. Cao surmised.

Ms. Cao surely understood the necessity for the regulation?

Well, yes, but I think she was offended that the receptionist did not take her word that I was officially employed by the PRC with all rights and privileges pertaining thereto. And also, comrades — may I flatter myself to think, and to say it? — I believe her concern for me was quite sincere. I'm sure she might have argued that it was a waste of an expensive resource like a foreign expert for me to be incapacitated by a headache that a few simple pills or cups of tea would cure. Objectively the receptionist's dogmatic application of the policy was undermining exactly what the policy was instituted to insure: fair and rightful and economical distribution of health care. In my case, it was costing more, not less, to enforce the rule. This is exactly what drives people nuts about bureaucracies everywhere. Whether in Russia or Massachusetts, Albania or Kenya, rules first, common sense last. But all this aside, I felt that Ms. Cao genuinely wanted to relieve even my comparatively minor suffering and was embarrassed that a fussy bureaucrat prevented it. It was to redeem China in my eyes as well as to express her own concern, that the next day she brought me the hat.

Of course, I protested. The hat was too expensive, and I couldn't accept it.

She noted the *fait accompli,* that it was a Western hat she could not readily give to anyone else, that it was for the good of the work unit that my health be maintained, that it was just my size, that I had already given her a sweater. . . .

What could I say? I accepted it then with genuine gratitude. The fact is that I would have never chosen such a hat for myself, since it was a bit sporty, you see, a bit, well, *young,* I thought, but it proved to be just the ticket. Narrow brimmed, skull tight, it would not too readily blow off as I cycled (except on the exceptional day already recounted), it was light and cool and folded up readily into book bag or suit coat pocket. That hat and I grew to be quite good friends, odd as that may sound. And I may as well confess this also: when I put the hat on, I thought of Ms. Cao, and that was a pleasure. It moved me that she had taken the time and the care — and money — to procure it, and when I put it on I thought of her hands touching it, evaluating it, selecting it, carrying it.

So you see, comrades, the hat came at a critical time. I had been away from America, and my wife, for more than two months. Daily I had worked with Ms. Cao and she seemed to me attractive and complicated and needy and sensitive and tough all at once. Sometimes when I returned to the hotel and shut the door and was alone, I would think of her with a kind of fondness I had not known for a very long time. And although she had done absolutely nothing to provoke such sentiments, I also sometimes thought of her with desire — the natural outcome of my sudden bachelorhood, to some extent, but to some extent also the inevitable result of being so close to such a beautiful woman for so much time. At my age, I know that such desire is not unusual, and also that it has no imperatives, can be readily mastered and kept secret. Any confession of sexual interest, I assumed, would be traumatic to our working relationship and might even destroy the uncomplicated and pleasant friendship we now enjoyed.

In America I suppose one would say I had a secret crush on Ms. Cao, fifteen years younger than me, and married, as I was and am, and I felt a little stupid when I found myself wishing for a more intimate connection with her.

Comrades! At that time, she had not once been to the You Yi Bing Guan. In fact I believe it fair to say that we had never been truly alone. On occasions we worked together in the office, "alone" when others left their desks; we had lunches together, surrounded by Beijingers; we traveled in the work unit taxi "alone", except for the taxi driver. We might have had opportunities to talk, that is, in English, which secured some of our conversation from eavesdroppers, but in China privacy is so nearly impossible that the concept is often not understood, let alone its desirability. Newlyweds frequently inhabit the dwellings of the groom's parents. On the train you sleep six to a cabin. In the office, we had three desks and one computer for use by nine people.

It should not have surprised me that even someone as self-possessed as Chen Tai-pan did not know how to be alone — indeed might even have been frightened by the prospect.

We expect a full accounting of your relationship to Chen Tai-pan.

I am aware of this, comrades.

When can we expect the details?

I don't know! I'm just not ready. I feel like hell about all that. Don't you know what grief is, for Christ's sake?

Then please tell us about the girl on the bicycle, who returned your hat.

That's no easier. I'm not talking any more today.

Then you will write it, as usual.

I don't know what I'll do today. Maybe just hang myself.

We will post a guard.

Ching nimen gei wo Beijing Pijiu ma?

Yes, if you continue, we will send out for some Beijing Beer. But you must go on.

May I tell you why I prefer Beijing Beer to Wu Sying?

How can it possibly be pertinent?

If a hat is pertinent, so is beer.

Then please proceed!

3

AMONG THE MEMBERS OF THE UNB — United Nations of Barflies, remember? — was a Canadian engineer named Kirby Cashman. When I met him the first week I arrived, Kirby had already been in China for about three months. He had contracted for a year's tour with a unit that was exploring economical and safe food processing. Kirby had had plenty of experience, everything from building bridges to automobile manufacture, but his last job in Canada had been with a brewery where he had learned a lot about, and devised machinery to create sturdy but light, cheap but attractive, easily packaged and stackable beer cans. It was this last item on Kirby's résumé that most interested your comrades at Beijing Food Canning. They wanted Kirby's help in the important business of food preservation — canned goods being, as you know, comparatively rare in China, making it necessary for too many people to make daily forays for the fresh food in stock and limiting significantly the variety of foods available in the winter months.

Now, given Kirby's professional concerns, it was not surprising that he was something of a fanatic about cleanliness. He was himself always quite nattily dressed in pin-stripe, button-down shirts and jackets that were nicely fitted to his slender, athletic form. His hair was curly, reddish-blonde, and he sported a matching beard. His eyes were the eyes of a hawk, intensely blue and penetrating, and I'm sure that any casual observer would have considered him quite a stunning, handsome fellow.

Alas, he was seething. Ten minutes in the glare of those hot blue eyes and you knew: he was breaking down. He was frightened to death of catching hepatitis. He imagined the Chinese in his division were trying to poison him, and he was scraping the food they brought him into a hole in the floor. He would start long monologues in the middle of someone else's conversation, and reach out suddenly and grip you in his talons and demand your attention if he felt you were trying to ignore him.

Which, increasingly, we all did. And the reason was not so much Kirby's constant lecturing — he was mad all right, but he was so full of incredible, sad information that was readily verifiable and therefore *fascinating* sometimes if also overwhelming — but that he had begun to grow violent, and very unpredictable. If his madness had stayed on the level of his painful, insightful haranguing, we all could have managed, but one night he threw himself across the table onto the throat of a young

British fellow who had been teasing him and ordering him to be quiet, and it took quite a few of us far too long to unclench Kirby's hands from the Brit's throat and drag him off. He was possessed of that special, demonic power that only madmen seem to have, and black eyes and bruises were displayed continuously for weeks whenever the subject of "Krazy Kirby's" attack was broached.

A tall, gentle poet with brooding eyes from California said this: "You know what Kirby's trouble is? He knows too much."

He was right. Among the things that Kirby knew were the rates of icemelt from the polar regions, and therefore when the coastal cities would be doomed by flood; he knew exactly to what degree our protective ozone layer was being eaten away by fluorocarbons and when, therefore, our food crops would shrivel in deadly ultraviolet rays; he knew how many atomic — "thermonuclear", he called them — warheads existed on the globe and declared the possibility of accident to be well over 100 per cent; he knew the rate at which petrochemical resources were being exhausted, and, since no one was seriously developing energy alternatives, predicted oil wars of massive proportions; he often discussed the impact of fossil fuel emissions on the atmosphere — evident in the sulfurous smell of every Chinese city, because of the ready availability of and necessity to burn coal; he was a mine of statistics on population growth, which he compared readily with dwindling supplies of arable land; and he was an encyclopedia in general of rapidly evolving planetary disasters of every stamp, from rain forest depletion to the murderous effects of acid rain.

"Civilization!" he would exclaim. "What about the flip side?"

Kirby also knew that many beers are made artificially buoyant by the addition of "foaming agents". This information came forth when the managers of the café in Building N° 1 decided to stop serving the beloved Beijing Beer and substituted instead the more expensive Chinese export brew, Wu Sying. We had all liked Beijing Beer for being honest and robust, and admittedly also for being cheap and coming in large and mighty green bottles — a lot more good brew for the buck. In grousing over the substitution, invidious comparisons were noted. Wu Sying, for example, was the world's foamiest beer. You poured it into a glass — Canadian journalists measured the exact proportions — and were left with about 2/3 foam and 1/3 beer. Someone speculated that the Chinese had heard that Westerners judged a beer by its head and had created a monster of excess. It was then that Krazy Kirby informed us about foaming agents in general.

"And the foaming agent in Wu Sying," he declared, laughing his absurd existential laugh, and nodding vigorously as if he knew we wouldn't believe this preposterous truth, "is cobalt."

We protested this assertion wildly.

"It's true," Kirby insisted. "But don't worry. You have to drink twenty cans a day for it to be an immediate hazard."

At this news, several of the journalists turned pale. Twenty cans! For some, this was a plausible daily ration.

"And why not?" Kirby continued. "The Chinese still use mercury and lead in their paints. Yes, they do. How do you think they achieve that noble red on the pillars in the Forbidden City and all the latest restorations? Mercury gives it that deep, imperial luster. Compare the Japanese temples. They're downright orange by comparison because mercury is outlawed there and they can't create this traditional color without it."

"Cut it out, Kirby! For Christ's sake!" someone urged.

"And insecticides! Sure, they kill the bugs all right. But these people are still using pure DDT in massive doses on vegetables and grain crops, and you know what that means."

"Don't tell us, Kirby, we beg you," said the man in the HAPPY OUR sweater. "Don't tell us our Wu Sying is ten parts cobalt and ten parts DDT."

"Parts per million, I wouldn't be surprised," Kirby said.

"Fisher," HAPPY OUR pleaded with me, "can't you do something to stop this fellow's outpouring of utterly morbid facts?"

"Me?" I was astounded to be singled out as having the slightest influence on Krazy Kirby's verbal peregrinations.

"He won't listen to any of the rest of us. You're our last resort."

"Well," I said, "we can always choose not to believe him. I notice we are still foaming at the cup, so to speak, and drinking it down."

"But the *rate*," HAPPY OUR said, "the *rate* of intake is distinctly slower. And now I don't know if I'm just getting nicely drunk or if parts of my brain are being destroyed."

Kirby laughed. "Your brain was destroyed a long time ago."

"You don't understand, do you?" HAPPY OUR said to Kirby. "There are some things in this life, many things which we'd rather not know."

"That's why we're doomed," Kirby said at once. "Nobody gives a shit." He smugly crossed his arms and pursed his lips, looking belligerent as hell.

It wasn't long after I'd been here in China, either, when Kirby latched onto me one evening and was following me to my building, gabbing away as I nearly dashed for cover. The walks were unlighted and the passage made treacherous by repairs to the grounds that were being carried on in preparation for the tourist season. Some of the walkways had been blocked off completely, and construction areas sealed off by six foot walls of bricks laid herring-bone fashion, held together by gravity only. I recall that it was a cold, drizzling night late in February, and the grounds in their disrepair with the carts and tricycles of the repairmen and the collected detritus of old, bent pipes and broken concrete and random piles of splintered boards and gravel were a drag on the spirit. Some of the buildings were being renovated and their windows had been broken out and they gaped like empty eye sockets in a skull. Kirby was meanwhile asking some penetrating questions about myself that I was in no mood to answer forthrightly. But finally he demanded:

"So why? Why did you come to China?"

I know now of course that this is the kind of question, will always be a question we cannot answer, not knowing our fates in advance, having no opportunity to rehearse our lives. But it was a question I had been asking myself, and the answer I was formulating would have been too personal to tell Kirby, too painful for me to express just then. Could I have said: "I came to China to fall in love?" "I came to China to fall prey to my own greed?" "I came to China to escape the killing boredom of my American life?" Could I have said any of these things and sounded less mad than Kirby himself?

And so I said simply, "I want to look around."

Kirby laughed at this, a low, dark laugh of amusement and appreciation. He formed his hand into a mock gun and fired at me. "That's good," he said. "I like that." The wind had picked up so that it made his beard quiver as I could see in the lights from the building windows when we reached civilized ground. We said nothing more. He stood like a statue in that chill drizzle, hands clasped behind his back, and watched me as I pushed through the revolving door into Building Nº 4. I don't know why, but I made double sure the door to my room was locked that night.

About two weeks later, Kirby got into an awful, violent row — threw chairs! — with a wonderful man from Nigeria I knew only as M'Bele and a Japanese fellow he was friendly with, Ozaku, whom I did not know very well but who liked to sport a baseball cap even in winter and who was reputed to have the best stash of Western classical music tapes of anyone in China. The violence brought one of the UNB to her senses, and then us to all of ours, at last.

"We've got to get him out of here," Edith Tilden said. "We've got to go to the Canadian Embassy and tell them this man is cracking up, he needs help, and he needs to go home." Edith, who taught English at one of the city's universities, was one of M'Bêle's close friends, and she was writing her dissertation on the black poets of South Africa. Don't, just don't ask me what she was doing in China under the circumstances. She had also been debilitated by some Chinese disease, but was recovering, and it should be obvious from her sensible suggestion that she was the only one among us with any sense left — due, perhaps, to her absolute scorn for the Wu Sying on the tables, and her insistence on drinking nothing but the finest brandy, damn the expense. But since the main thrust of her discourse heretofore had been to vilify South Africa and England in equal measure and Western civilization generally, this note of compassion for our mad colleague struck us all with special force. We had not particularly appreciated the motherly side of Edith before, and I think we were all a little ashamed that we had not each of us reached this common sense resolution to help Krazy Kirby on our own. So of course it became a cause.

Comrades! I am sure you have heard about our efforts to free Krazy Kirby from his duties and ship him home for counseling and succor. Some of you may even have been called in to advise on what could be done to unsnarl him from contractual arrangements or to expedite the bureaucratic processes for his release. His rescue from China, from himself.

I saw him walk by the building this morning, cracking his knuckles as he ogled the nurses who had come outside in their white uniforms and caps to do some calisthenics to music on the lawn. He stood there watching them with a cynical grin on his face, every once in a while lifting himself on his toes and sticking out his chin, rather like a rooster. Then his head snapped around and he looked right at me, directly into the window. Still here. He seemed to be offended that I would be observing him. Edith Tilden is gone, the California poet is gone, HAPPY OUR is somewhere in Thailand I've heard, but of my generation of experts in Beijing, it's just me and Krazy Kirby who are left. We do not drink Wu Sying beer.

4

For the moment, we must regard your last remarks as a digression. May we remind you that the fates of several people are entwined with yours and your delaying tactics affect many people? Today we insist that you deal strictly with your familiarity with the girl who returned your cap. Lay your feelings aside, however preciously you may hold them, and do this work. This is very important.

Lay my feelings aside? Oh, I like that, comrades! Of course it is the most decadent, bourgeois thing of all to savor one's emotions, to wallow in them. And it's true, you know, that all through my life I have been a victim of cloudy thinking, have been unable to muster the discipline to see things, and act objectively, according to the real situation, conditions, facts of the matter. Let's not play at this any longer. Let me become clear and disciplined.

I know that you know who Tai Hai-yan is. I know that you have a self-criticism from her, just as you have a self-criticism from Cao Song-wen, or are in the process of squeezing one out of her, and another from our dear taxi driver, Wen Da-xing, and who knows who else. Objectively speaking, it would of course be quite difficult for you to have a self-criticism from Chen Tai-pan, since he is dead, but it will be interesting to note when this is all over whether or not a convenient diary doesn't materialize. I wonder what functionary would take upon himself the task of writing the dead Chen Tai-pan's diary for the gratification of the prosecution. Will he throw in any little emotional tidbits to suggest the flaws in his character? We know, for example, that Chen Tai-pan liked flowers. Please! Be sure to inform your writer of Chen Tai-pan's ersatz diary that once he and I walked together with Tai Hai-yan, the beautiful young woman who returned my hat, under a canopy of purple wisteria and the two of them — shameful thought! — quoted poetry to each other from Chinese classics, and then explained (or tried to) the poems to me. Or perhaps that is exactly what you would expect of three criminals like ourselves.

I think of that moment now and there are certain unmentionable feelings associated with it, some kind of insipid nostalgia, some wicked grief, a no doubt evil sorrow, even some nauseating happiness. Purple wisteria blossoms! Poetry! A beautiful girl! Of all the cheap tricks!

Tai Hai-yan was about five feet six inches tall, weighing about 112 pounds. She was educated in Hunan at a secretarial college, but since she demonstrated exceptional abilities was transferred to Beijing Managerial Training Institute. I forget the details of her résumé, but, comrades, you may insert them here. Blah blah blah. The record will show that she fulfilled the expectations of her former teachers in Hunan and graduated blah blah blah. I'm sure you have all this information.

Tai Hai-yan had sad brown eyes. No. Get rid of the "sad". She had utterly exquisite lips. No. Get rid of the utterly exquisite. She had two lovely, firm breasts. Stop that! Be objective. She had two breasts. This was ascertained, comrades, by careful counting. One, two. There were no breasts in between, above or below the two counted, or anywhere else on her person or in her belongings. Though it is pure speculation on my part, I believe experience suggests that she had no other breasts at her work unit, or in her dormitory, or at the homes of her various relatives in either Beijing or Zhenzhou.

She also had two feet, two legs, two thighs, and — oh, comrades! — I am sorry, but I cannot without emotion think of her feet and legs and between her legs and her rump and her two breasts and tight belly, and beautiful clean neck, and two lips — yes, two! one on top of the other — none of this without emotion. I tried. I failed.

You see, after she rode off the morning Ms. Cao and our taxi driver, Wen Da-xing, were loading watermelons, I never expected to see her again. And truthfully, I was quite smitten with her, from her physical beauty to the lovely sound of her voice, the laughter that was hidden in it just below the surface, as if this were a person who could enjoy things, new things, who could be delighted. I consider this a very special gift, and rare. It actually made me sad to see her ride off on that morning. But of course I had plenty of other things on my mind, including watermelons.

Let me try to follow your instructions, comrades, and try to focus on Tai Hai-yan, even though Cao Song-wen and Wen Da-xing are now driving around in this narrative with a carload of watermelons and have yet to find a place to deliver them.

Be objective: my heart rate has increased. My palms are sweaty. I am sure my temperature is higher now. All of these reactions occur whenever I think of Tai Hai-yan. Sometimes there is another reaction, but comrades, after all, have you *no* imagination?

To be completely honest and to eschew any and all obfuscation of the matter henceforth: comrades, I loved Tai Hai-yan as I have loved no other woman in my life. I loved her passionately, unrestrainedly, holistically.

And yet, a) I never did anything she did not first request, and b) I never, ever achieved what I most desired. Furthermore, I want to insist that this was a matter of lust only in the most incidental way, but was primarily and steadfastly a romance — perhaps the only true, and perhaps the last romance of my life.

Comrades! I'm sorry. I must lay down a moment.

Apparently you fell asleep.

I hate sleeping with my clothes on. I slept badly. I had terrible dreams. I dreamed you were holding Tai Hai-yan under arrest.

We are not interested in your dreams.

Well, you should be . . . comrades. I know you feel Freud is bunk, and I agree, but only to a point. Dream life *is* revealing.

We are only interested in your actions, the sequence of events leading to Chen Tai-pan's murder.

Am I being accused of murder, comrades?

That determination has yet to be made.

Good God! Does the Embassy know you are holding me?

Yes.

Good God!

You must continue. We must have all the facts.

I have a terrible headache today. I don't want to write anything. I feel I'm betraying my friends and lovers.

You were telling us about your romance with Tai Hai-yan. Well?

May I please have some aspirin?

Of course.

It kills me to think I may never see her again, you know. And after all, it was me who corrupted her, who got her involved with the bicycles.

First tell us about Tai Hai-yan and then tell us about the bicycles.

Well, the two stories kind of go together anyway. Greed, you know, is a lousy fundament for any action. You know *The Treasure of the Sierra Madre?* Read it. It's the truth. You ought to show that movie around Beijing. Myself, I should have been satisfied with watermelons and said to hell with the bicycles, and most of all I should have kept Tai Hai-yan out of it. I mean, really, comparatively, she was just a kid! I'm twenty years older, I'm turning her into a hustler of bicycles. How could I do such a thing? How could she know I can't stand to see a good idea just wither and die?

For one thing, I guess I was curious about what she would do with a little spending money. I didn't think it would corrupt her — she wasn't going to be making enough to buy Jaguars in Beijing, and even if she did, where would she find one? where could she drive it? where the hell could she even park it? — but I was curious to see what money would bring out of her, how she would express herself in dollars. Comrades, do you know what she did with the first 240 *kuai* she made? She went out and bought a camera. She bought film. I showed her how to put film in the camera. And then she took her first picture.

Of me!

But obviously, I need to back up a little, don't I?

One evening before dinner, I was drying my toes — I remember this because I had heard someone boast that China had eliminated athlete's foot, and there I was with a dose and feeling like a leper about it, bringing such a scourge to the East. We have a terrible cultural guilt about such things because we learn now in our history books that it was not only racism and failure of cultural cross-communication that doomed the Indians in America, but tuberculosis (because they had developed no antibodies to it) and alcohol poisoning. There are lessons in this, I presume. I know you fear AIDS, as everyone should, and require your foreign experts to be certified free of it. Odd, but I don't remember Krazy Kirby mentioning AIDS. Perhaps it was just one thing too many to be packed into his sorrowful cerebral encyclopedia of disasters.

But there I was drying my toes, feeling guilty about bringing my particular germ pool along with me to the Orient, and also obliged, in my near naked state, to assess the damage of my decadent Western life on my ideal physical self, there being about a ten *jin* (twenty pound) discrepancy. Such reflections were perhaps accentuated by the loneliness of hotel life. The telephone rang. Or rather, it exploded. This was such a rare event that the sound was psychologically magnified, I'm sure, but I am also sure, comrades, that it is scientifically verifiable that in pure decibels alone, the Chinese phone alarm is surely the world's most powerful. I must say it always reminded me of the bells which clangored away in the elementary school I attended to alert the entire world to the end of our class periods. Now, of course, the sound has an ominous ring of prison to it, the alarm preceding the final lock-up of the day. (We see lots of prison movies in America. All of us think we know what the inside of a prison is like.)

Self-absorbed as I was in my petty vanities and trifling guilts, I had no idea that fate was calling. Perhaps you Chinese are absolutely right to have decided on so imperious a cry from your telephones, to alert us that every call is the result of a network of decisions, a desire for communication, and, hence, an event of at least potential substance.

Yes, this was Tai Hai-yan's first call. She had been cycling by the You Yi Bing Guan and on a whim dismounted, showed the card I had given her to the guards at the gate, who rang me up and asked if I were expecting her. I had no inkling who "Tai Hai-yan" was, but if someone wanted to see me and had my card, I was curious to know whom, and why. Any scoundrel could have come through the gates that way, you're right. I quickly tossed on some clothes, picked up the newspapers and towels scattered here and there in a bid to appear semi-civilized, and when I opened the door to the timid knocking, I did not at first realize who was standing there.

She laughed when she saw the look on my face, and said, "Please. I like to buy hat. Is this hat shop?"

Well, I was quite bowled over. This was the hat girl, all right, athletic yet feminine, her roundish face calm behind thick glasses, with those incredible lips! And wearing another bright skirt — this one a coral color with dark lozenges. I invited her in, served her a cup of tea. She sat in one of my two chairs, legs crossed, very prim, and yet delighted about something, seemed in fact on the verge of laughing out loud.

"What amuses you so?" I asked. "You've never seen a foreign expert before?"

"I never talk to American before," she said. Then she struggled to communicate that although she had cycled past the You Yi Bing Guan all her life and often wondered what it was like inside the fences — she had heard tales of swimming pools, billiard tables, dances — she never imagined she would someday pass through the gates.

"Well, you're in luck," I said. "I'll take you to dinner, and then I'll give you a walking tour of the grounds."

She refused the dinner, saying she felt improperly dressed and would be too shy among so many foreigners. Alas, I could find no way to prevail upon her to stay and when she finished her tea, she left. And after she left, comrades, I seemed to feel this incredible vacuum where she had just been, almost as if she had walked off with one of my internal organs. I actually sat in the chair she had been in and savored the lingering warmth. At least we had made arrangements to meet the coming Saturday at the Beijing Art Museum, to see an exhibit of photographs of China by a Japanese artist sponsored by Mobil Oil — ah, the modern world! — and for the rest of the week I was quite giddy with anticipation.

I imagine ours was not the first romance to take root in the Beijing Art Museum, under the glittering panels of Wang Wei's cherry blossoms, say. At least this is where the romance began for me, with the clear realization that my interest was well beyond the fatherly and possibly also not completely devoid of hope. Tai Hai-yan had nothing also of the fortune-hunter about her, nothing of the passport-hunter, nothing the least bit sinister or even insincere. Without that little spark of hope, of course, I could have closed my heart again, and kept it sealed. I was practiced at it.

Tai Hai-yan was frank about her feelings, her desires and goals. In spite of our linguistic limitations, we found much in common, and communicated profoundly. Tai Hai-yan's lack of inhibition about herself was so refreshing! Weary to death of the circumspection and circumlocution of most of the other Chinese I knew, I thought Hai-yan clear-sighted, honest, forthright — and she seemed to enjoy being able to be so, and perhaps my being American is what inspired this in her.

Months later when we had become quite close friends, she remarked, "I'm such different person with you! I'm more like I wish myself."

She echoed my feelings precisely. I don't know why, but she made me want to be gentle and generous, and I felt so many of my psychological calluses had been dissolved by her influence, so that many things I would not have noticed before now seemed fresh and wonderful.

My lotus!

I will never forgive you, comrades, if you have her in prison.

You are not in a position to be forgiving.

Why are you threatening me now? Frankly, I don't see that you are in a position to demand anything. I want a lawyer.

Mr. Fisher, we are the lawyers.

You're *what?*

Please continue to tell us about Tai Hai-yan. Please at once. Mr. Sun will soon bring some Beijing Beer for you. Then you can have a rest.

Take a rest. I don't know how many times I have corrected Tai Hai-yan on the same locution. That's something I rediscovered with her that I had also discovered with Ms. Cao — that I am too impatient to be a really good teacher. I hate to do things twice, to give instructions twice, say, repeat myself, correct the same mistakes more than once. This naturally makes me a complete hypocrite, comrades, because I certainly expect most people to give me three strikes before I'm called out. Even worse, if I correct the speech of Tai Hai-yan, I expect your speech to have been corrected, too. The few times I have had to grade papers or tests, you see, or even to oversee the exercises of my computer students — I call this hell, comrades, finding and correcting the same mistakes over and over again.

Am I as hard on myself? I believe so.

This may explain why, in the watermelon and bicycle operations, I hired only the best workers and the brightest, quickest people. I want to give explanations and orders only once, and to have them carried out without quibbling over details. I don't mind reasonable questions or helpful criticism, but I fire quibblers.

Now Tai Hai-yan was an exceedingly quick student. She went through grammar books like you and I would kill a platter of dumplings. (By the way, comrades, what are the chances of some *jao zi* some evening?) I'm lucky if I learn ten new Chinese words a week — a month! — let's be honest. Tai Hai-yan would learn ten new English words at breakfast, ten at lunch, ten at supper. I had known her a month and she was reading Erich Segal's *Love Story;* three months and she was laughing and crying aloud over Dickens. To this day — what? eighteen months in China? — I still can't read *The People's Daily.* If she hadn't made me feel so wonderful in other ways, I'm afraid that being around Tai Hai-yan would mainly have made me feel old and stupid.

And not just clever. She really seemed to have a sixth sense of how other people felt and thought about things; she was proud of herself, and yet not at all vain; and she seemed to balance better than anyone I've ever known talking about herself or other things she knew about, and listening. Sometimes, as we all are, she was sullen or unhappy, but most of the time she conveyed a quality of mirth, of enjoying life, of barely concealed delight and surprise with what life could dish up — and out! She certainly had her share of hard knocks, poor kid! They sent her father out west to cut trees during the cultural revolution and he damned near starved to death, came back terribly ill and Hai-yan had to nurse him along whenever she wasn't in school. During the same time, she and her mother were sent to Tianjin to raise pigs on a rice growing commune, and the only education she received was from her mother, and that in secret. The crimes of her parents had been quite serious to warrant such treatment: they were "intellectuals". They had been Russian teachers!

Which brings me back to the You Yi Bing Guan, and Tai Hai-yan, and bicycles.

Oh, boy. Read carefully, comrades!

As you know, the You Yi Bing Guan was the residence of the Russian foreign experts long before it was the residence of the Western UNB. In fact, as any fool can tell, the Ruskies built the place, I think on the model of a train station, which they then topped with some Chinese sloping, tile roofs — the only detail besides the beautiful landscaping which saves the place from looking like a factory compound. And when the fallout between Russia and China came, the Russian experts piled out of here in a panic, a mad rush. Oh, they took enough time to destroy everything they could lay hands on first, but the last thing on their minds was their — bicycles! Yes!

Now the Ruskies had kept their own bicycles in a little, covered parking area, and there they stayed, gathering dust and rusting a little, doing no one any harm or any good, either, and because they were inside the foreign compound, escaped — miraculously! — becoming the property of the people of Beijing.

One day Tai Hai-yan and I returned from a bicycle ride to a local park and because it was just beginning to rain a little, we were stashing our bicycles under an archway in a futile attempt to keep them dry.

"Why you don't keep bike over there?" she asked, pointing to the sheltered bicycle lot.

"It's too crowded," I said. "I can never find a space."

"Those bikes are too old!" she said. "Nobody ride those."

To tell the truth, it had never dawned on me before that what she said was true. Later, I strolled through the shed and discovered the old Ruskie bikes with their fat tires and wide fenders and little odds and ends in the baskets — even a desiccated bouquet of flowers and a crumbling, Russian newspaper. It was a genuine bicycle graveyard! And, capitalist in spirit as I apparently am, remembering the great difficulty I had in obtaining a bike for myself and the terrific demand that exists for them everywhere in China, it crossed my mind that a fellow with a few wrenches and some grease and oil and a little ingenuity could probably make a few *kuai* selling off refurbished ghost bicycles! And that, one fine day, was the task I set for Tai Hai-yan.

One day she was complaining bitterly about the cost of taking the TEFL exam, the foreign language exam you need to pass for a passport here — thirty dollars US, about 120 *kuai,* six weeks' salary for her. To take a test she could flunk! Of course I loaned her the money, but you Chinese are very scrupulous about loans, as bad as any Jew or Yankee farmer on that score — debts being for all concerned a moral taint, a disease even. Consequently, Tai Hai-yan wished aloud she could make more money to unburden herself from the deep debt I had thrown her into, among other things.

So I said to her, "O.K. I know where you can get 186" (I had counted them) "used bicycles for nothing. They need to be fixed up, and they may need some parts. I'd be willing to pay someone to fix those bicycles and someone to sell them, if I could turn a little profit. You follow me?"

She followed me, comrades, and she thought the idea was outrageous, unscrupulous, unfair. I asked why. I said no one owned the bicycles. They were salvage. We would rescue them from idleness and decay. We would help supply the need (I said "need," I didn't say "demand") for bicycles, help, that is, in a small way to combat the bicycle shortage. What was her objection?

Now she faltered. She didn't quite like the idea of "salvage". She thought the bicycles should belong to someone.

"But the owners are gone," I said. "Surely many are even dead by now. The living ones couldn't get into the country even if they wanted to. The bikes are just sitting there, going to waste."

She was more persuaded now. She understood also the special value of the bicycles with their many baskets and bells, but, even more important, their special You Yi Bing Guan license plates, which identified them as either foreign expert bicycles or the bicycles of You Yi Bing Guan workers. With such a license plate, you could bicycle unmolested into and, more pertinent to our scheme, out of the You Yi Bing Guan compound without being stopped by the guards.

Tai Hai-yan, quick student as she was, noted that the license plates alone would be worth something in the wrong hands. Such innocence! Comrades, do you understand why I loved this woman? She never conceived the "wrong hands" could be her own!

When it was dark, Tai Hai-yan and I made an inspection of several of the ghost bicycles in the beam of my rechargeable flashlight. They indeed did look ghostly under their layers of pink dust, but we managed to shake one likely prospect loose and roll it to an open, paved area beside a utility shed. The chain and main gear were rusty, but nothing a wire brush couldn't improve in short order, or a little soaking in gasoline; the tires were soft, but the real rubber tires with their real rubber inner tubes were not as bad as you'd expect and we pumped these up using an air hose at the taxi stand; all the moving parts were dry, of course, but I took the liberty of draining a little oil from the crankcase of a tractor in a hotel construction area and applying it to the chain, brake cables, gears, bearings.

Then Tai Hai-yan took it for a little test spin, and by golly, I think that was the ride that convinced her that we could do business. Yes, the bike was sluggish, but she could see the possibilities, and she even confessed to liking the feel of that solid old machine, comfortable and honest in its heft, and she even liked the old-fashioned look of it, something different, something ... well ... individual, comrades, but not outrageously so.

I untangled another bicycle from the cluster of the old Russian behemoths, and after applications of a little more oil and air, Tai Hai-yan and I went off for a moonlight ride around the nine buildings of the You Yi Bing Guan. She even got her bell to work, though the one on my bike remained frozen. Easy to fix! The main thing was that these bikes were viable, repairable, usable, salable. No question about it!

We also made a second discovery. We pulled up to Building Nº 4 and were saying good night when one of those wonderful simultaneous revelations flooded over both our minds.

"With this bike," Tai Hai-yan said, leaning back to regard its license plate. . . .

"You could come and go from here without signing in all the time."

"Yes." She looked at me a little shyly, but also impishly.

"You take that bike," I said. "You try it out. We want to be sure we are going to be selling a quality product."

"But then I have two bike," she said. "That's too many!"

"One bike is the company bike," I said. I watched her look the old Russian bicycle over quite carefully. "What is it worth," I asked her, "just like it is right now, no fix-up?"

She shrugged. "Maybe forty, maybe fifty *kuai*."

"Fixed up, could we get a hundred for it?"

"Hundred!" she said. "Hundred fifty."

"Multiply that times one hundred and eighty six," I said.

"Eighteen thousand six hundred *kuai*," she said, eyes widening, "maybe even more than twenty-seven thousand *kuai!*"

"Do you think we can run a business with that?"

Tai Hai-yan laughed. "I do think so!"

Comrades! I take full responsibility. I unleashed a monster.

Tai Hai-yan queried a few of her colleagues at the petroleum refinery and it was immediately apparent that any number of used bicycles could be sold as quickly as they became available. One hundred and eighty-six bikes would hardly even dent the demand. Therefore, she began discreetly to ask around about a good bicycle mechanic, and went so far as to take her Russian Rider to one she had heard about to see what he would do with it. She was not satisfied, and tried another. Still not satisfied, she learned of a man at the refinery, a worker who had once been employed at the Datong Railway Factory making the world's last steam engines, and who was reputed not just to be a jack of all trades, but a kind of mechanical genius. She approached him — no doubt with the irresistible pout on her face — with a badly crippled Russian Rider, declaring it had sentimental value in her family, and asked if he could do something with it.

You may find this difficult to believe, comrades, but I never learned this man's name. I am ashamed of this fact, but it was just one of those names which doesn't stick in a foreigner's mind, filled as it was with the unfamiliar Chinese phonemes of *jr, zhr, dz, zi*. I took the route of cultural imperialism, I'm afraid, and called him "Whiz", and came also and eventually to think of him in my own mind as "Quick-as-Death". If I ever get out of here and it could somehow be arranged, I would love to take "Whiz" to America. He doesn't speak a scrap of English, but never mind that, there is absolutely nothing he doesn't understand the workings of, given ten minutes of tinkering, and can't cob a way to repair. Once he even repaired my electric typewriter, a device he had never even seen before.

Mr. Whiz turned one of our clunker Russian Riders into a nearly gleaming (not all the patina of age can be removed), easy-pedaling, bell-jangling, quick-stopping Russian Glider. When he was done with it, the bicycle practically pedaled itself, and Mr. Whiz showed that he understood something else, the kind of thing that persuaded Tai Hai-yan and me that he was not just a mechanic, but an artist: a tremendous difference is made in the very spirit of a machine when the nonfunctional details are given the same concern as the functional ones. That is, Tai Hai-yan's bicycle came back from Mr. Whiz with the factory emblem polished, new (red!) handle grips with matching seat cover, a gleaming bell, a basket that did not rattle, and reflectors that sparkled. (Believe this! The man had taken the reflectors apart, polished the interior chrome and washed the lenses! Consequently, the bike did not just sit there, but seemed to be looking at you, awaiting your command.)

Therefore, we hired Mr. Whiz. Of course he could not give up his job, and could only work in the evenings. He knew of a shed where we could deliver a few bicycles at a time, and he knew someone who could discreetly supply him with some of the repair parts and the accessories he would need to turn out a finished product. Of course I paid his salary and supplied the capital. When we got to know him well enough to know also that he was completely trustworthy, we brought him into the You Yi Bing Guan and showed him our trove of abandoned bicycles.

Shall I say, comrades, that when it became clear to him how much money he stood to make refurbishing bicycles, he became very enthusiastic? He broke out laughing when he saw all those bicycles waiting for resurrection, clapped his hands, laughed some more. When he regained a little sobriety, he pointed out (via Tai Hai-yan) that in fact there might be savings if we cannibalized a few of the bikes for parts rather than buying the parts new.

I tried to explain to him that this was a "false economy" in that, demand being so high, we did not have to attempt to make the bicycles inexpensive. We could pass the expenses on to the consumer.

Both Tai Hai-yan and Mr. Whiz had a little difficulty with this concept at first, but accepted my decision. Mr. Whiz's first act — the devil! — was quite properly to ask for a raise. Our labor negotiations were swift. I said "yes".

Now Tai Hai-yan and I were in the bicycle business. Naturally, I knew very well the You Yi Bing Guan guards were going to get suspicious about the increase in bicycle traffic and, license plates notwithstanding, could exercise their prerogative to stop any Chinese person coming through the gates. I might therefore have hired (or even tricked) some other foreign experts to be the bicycle delivery system, but I was quite jealous of our business idea and didn't want to risk its becoming public information, and I also wanted to keep the enterprise small, to avoid diluting profits any more than necessary. (Making jobs, you see, was not my priority — another capitalist maneuver.) Therefore, I invented a little stratagem that, as it turned out, worked very nicely indeed.

I made sure that whenever Mr. Whiz or Tai Hai-yan wheeled a bicycle out of the You Yi gates, they carried in their baskets either a few handfuls of straw concealing a brick (considerable construction was in progress on the grounds and these were easy to obtain) or a paper bag containing anything at all that was comparatively innocent, but also a little extravagant by Chinese standards and which would have to be paid for with Foreign Exchange Certificates rather than the people's *renminbi*.

Mr. Whiz was the first to be stopped and searched, and the brick was discovered in the straw. Obviously he was stealing bricks to fix up his cottage, the guards reasoned, and decided to look the other way. After all, Mr. Whiz was only stealing from foreigners! What were a few bricks to them or anyone else? Beijing, called "The City of Bicycles" might as well be called "The City of Bricks" since almost everything is built from them.

Tai Hai-yan was eventually stopped as well, and did the perfectly correct thing in demanding that they keep their hands off her paper bag.

Aha! An American magazine.

Aha! A can of Wu Sying beer.

To keep them from filing a complaint, Tai Hai-yan sacrificed the Wu Sying.

In short order, Mr. Whiz and Tai Hai-yan became quite familiar to the guards. They winked at Mr. Whiz as he cycled by with his brick; they occasionally stopped Tai Hai-yan, I'm sure just to enjoy looking at her, but also occasionally to check the paper bag. It was learned the beer of choice was San Miguel.

And so the bicycle business prospered.

And will prosper, comrades, quite independent of us, because I believe that out of my capitalist, perhaps opportunistic impulse there emerged something quite unexpected and for which a demand will exist for a long time: Mr. Whiz's limited edition, collector's item bicycle. My spies tell me that they recently heard of the sale of one, with its distinctive red handle grips, for more than 200 *kuai* — not much less than a new bike would cost and a nearly 20 per cent appreciation in only what? four months? or is it five now? since the bicycle business ended.

As for our personal relationship, comrades, between Tai Hai-yan and I, this also prospered. She visited me several times a week and my attraction to her was so apparent that it quickly ceased to be a secret. I'm sure being co-conspirators in the bicycle business had much to do with it, but we were friendly in the most free-wheeling way I've ever known, leaping on every impulse, and yet Tai Hai-yan at least maintained the discipline of her English study and of running her business as well.

One Sunday she came by to pick up a bicycle, yes, but also to watch my television, the Sunday English program. The television was in the bedroom atop a huge, round table with a pink tablecloth on it, underneath which, if anyone had looked, would have been discovered a vast number of ten *kuai* notes, the largest denomination made at that time, profits from the bicycle and watermelon trade. I couldn't begin to tell you how much money was there. I didn't count it, simply stashed it. Anyone could have lifted half of it and I wouldn't have known the difference. Maybe someone did! I certainly hope so!

Typically, Tai Hai-yan came on Sundays to watch the English program (although there was a television in her dormitory, her comrades preferred to watch the volleyball matches or whatever), and I would toss some pillows on the bed so that she could sit there comfortably, and then I would either pull up a chair, or go off to my desk and prepare for Monday's work. But on this day, after I had produced some pillows and she had made herself comfortable, she patted the mattress beside her and said, "Arnold. Why you don't sit here?"

I knew the reason quite well, comrades, and you do, too. If I sat close, quite likely I would not be able to keep my hands off her. Which is precisely what happened. I had been sexually starved in any case, and then to find myself next to this Chinese dream — well, it was impossible.

And the response, comrades, was rather dull at first, and she leaned her chin over my shoulder to be able to continue watching television as I stroked and fondled and touched and kissed and gently squeezed and began to excite myself even if she remained sluggish in spirit, narcotized by some backstage glimpse into the life of a Western ballerina, possibly even some Russian defector. Perhaps Tai Hai-yan could tell you the program content on that day, but it was lost on me.

Soon enough, however, we were quite passionately kissing each other and sharing groans of inflamed desire. She was not a practiced kisser, comrades, and it's quite possible that her tongue was a virgin as the rest of her was — and in the most fundamental way is yet. Though it had seemed to me that we had made the standard rate of progress toward the usual end — speaking as an American male, you see — and although my friend had made no objection whatsoever to any of my foreplay forays and gave every sign to my middle-aged Western eyes, ears, nose, tongue, fingers and toes of being wholly receptive to consummating our physical relationship, well, when it came just precisely the perfect moment to insert unit A into unit C, when, that is, I had imagined myself about to achieve an absolutely unimaginable prize in my life on this often disappointing planet, and when I had at last thrown off all guilts and inhibitions relating to my dear wife at home — a terrible chill.

"No," she said. "No, no no."

"No?" I said. "No?"

"Don't want baby," she said.

"Of course." I shifted to remove unit A from any closer contact with unit C, and with her guidance substituted a pair of digits where unit A still clamored to be admitted.

Now, in this state we had a long talk about a subject we should have discussed long before. I presumed I could obtain some prophylactics from my work unit health clinic, or even from the hotel clinic which was close by. I was told I could do as I liked in that respect, but "Arnold, please try to understand something." My heart sank at the tone of her voice. Of course! How could I have been so stupid not to realize that there was someone else — had to be someone else, this woman being so young, bright, altogether remarkable.

"No, there is not someone else." She told me she had once been engaged, but her fiancé was transferred to a work unit in another city and had quickly found another sweetheart. She had not made love to him or any other man, and for the same reason that she didn't want to make love to me: she wanted to be a virgin on her wedding night, to give her virginity to the man with whom she would have her one legal child.

In America, it is true, we still hear of such things, and there are even people who applaud such a decision. Under the precise circumstances already alluded to, however, such a declaration of principle might not always be taken seriously, at least not at that precise moment in the process, when a man's hearing is likely to be impaired. Remember also that while I was being informed of this resolute principle, unit C was displaying a most heart-stopping degree of activity, including the copious production of fluids, among other sweet things, and unit A was craning its little neck and head in desperate search of almost any cover for its nakedness. Moral philosophy at such moments is exceedingly poignant, I hope you agree.

Even so, there was no question in my mind that I would play by Tai Hai-yan's rules. I may be a capitalist and an adventurer, but I hope I am not an exploiter and under no circumstances a rapist. Decadent as I may be, I nevertheless have scruples that limit the barbarities I will commit and the advantages I seek. And I'm sure I've explained sufficiently already that lust was not the main factor in my attraction to this woman, real as that factor was, but a real tenderness, a real desire to do the best for her, to be the best possible companion under the constraints of our hot-house China life.

Blind, stupid, easily fooled by substitutes, unit A eventually earned an ersatz relief.

Oh! And I'd promised to be objective!

We see no reason for tears, Mr. Fisher.

Not even tears of repentance?

Here is your Beijing Beer. Please continue.

All right.

5

As for the watermelon business, I had better make it clear, I think, how I came to be involved, some of the problems which arose, and some of the relationships which developed from it. At last I will have to say something about dear Chen Tai-pan.

I think the first thing to point out is that I was used in the watermelon affair, that I entered into it quite naively, and trusted people I really didn't know very well. I certainly did not know that at the moment I began to supply money for the operation, a deep structure was already in place, stretching all the way to Russia and involving Xinjiang money-changers and a whole network of Silk Road hanky-panky, a secondary economy and organization existing inside the official one!

In other words, comrades, I was being played for a sucker and through my influence Ms. Cao got taken in, too.

Oh, I know you asked for a confession, comrades, and the statement I have just made suggests a line of attack rather than an admission of guilt — but it is, in fact, both. No doubt I participated in something nefarious which led to the most evil result of a wonderful man's death; but it is also true that I did not know what I was getting into or that such serious consequences were even a potential in the game.

Wen Da-xing, the work unit taxi driver, first broached the subject to me, in his wonderful Chinglish. Wen was chauffeuring me to the Beijing Hotel (one of my favorite places in town, by the way) where I was going to offer some suggestions on setting up a computer network to expedite airlines and railway ticket purchases. The summer was not far along and I was surprised to see suddenly huge mounds of watermelons for sale on street corner after street corner. The melons were smaller than the US version, ranging in size from that of a soccer ball to that of a football, and were clearly in public demand. I mentioned to Wen that I had never realized that the Chinese were such big consumers of watermelons, that it was not a food Americans associated with the Chinese at all.

"Very popular," Wen said. "Big money, too."

"Really?"

"Expensive!"

"And yet look at the crowds around those watermelon stands. Where do the melons come from?"

"*Xi gua,*" Wen said, "means 'west melon.' From Xinjiang, by train. Also very popular in Shanghai."

"Plenty popular right here, obviously."

"Big competition for melon," Wen said. "Maybe we have melon war."

"Really?"

"Hard to get extra melon to sell."

"Surplus melons, beyond state quotas, you mean?"

"Yes."

"That's fascinating," I said.

"If I have money," Wen said, rubbing his fingers together, "I can get plenty melon."

"Is that so?"

"True," Wen said. "I know people."

I didn't rise to this at the moment, but a seed, so to speak, had been planted. I asked the UNB about the watermelon phenomenon that evening and they assured me that watermelon was the hottest product in the country. People had been arrested for trying to steal melons in transit from the west to the coastal cities. Street vendors of melons actually got into fights over supplies.

Krazy Kirby, for once speaking to the topic at hand, informed us "In Shanghai, in the summer time, solid waste doubles, because of watermelon rinds."

"Learn to make something from watermelon rinds," HAPPY OUR, the chubby British journalist remarked, "and you'll be a national hero in China."

"My grandmother pickled them," M'Bele said, downing a Wu Sying. "Are the Chinese ready for that?"

Edith the scholar remarked, "They make vodka from potato skins, don't they? Couldn't something similar be done with rinds?"

"Vodka is not a Chinese communist priority," HAPPY OUR pointed out.

"Well, then," Edith persisted, "perhaps alcohol as fuel."

"Or maybe both," HAPPY OUR said. "A little for the tractor, a little for me."

"Let's not encourage drunk driving here," Edith responded. "Traffic's crazy enough."

As you have anticipated, I also queried Ms. Cao about the watermelon question. Oh yes, she said, it was a vastly important agricultural product, of great nutritional value, and she couldn't imagine a Chinese summer without it. Sharing a watermelon after a meal was a family, sometimes even a community rite.

Indeed all that summer it was for me (and not only because profits were involved) one of the greatest pleasures to be cycling at night down a dark street and then to come upon a cluster of people sitting on a curb, perhaps in the mellow glow of a one or two candlepower bulb, sharing a melon and talking in that amiable, bubbling, chuckling, near-whispering way that a watermelon and darkness seem to inspire. It made me think that when I returned to America I might do something really crazy and get into ice cream. What better things to sell than watermelons and ice cream? Though you don't like to hear such things, comrades, I even dreamed one night that I flew around the globe, like Santa Claus, parachuting milkshakes and watermelons everywhere I went. Free, of course.

What insanity!

Actually, in Beijing, our watermelons were being delivered by taxi, at least at first. And this is where Chen Tai-pan comes in.

No, not yet. Let Wen Da-xing and Ms. Cao drive around the block one more time. First things first.

From my conversation with the UNB and Ms. Cao about watermelons, it was pretty apparent to me that if a guy had a chance to purchase watermelons in quantity, as Wen Da-xing claimed he did, then he certainly ought to jump at it. I also asked Ms. Cao about this.

"I trust Wen," she said, "but I don't know about buying melons. You could get into trouble."

"But how would anyone know my money was involved?" I said.

Ms. Cao considered this. "I don't see any way to trace it," she said. "I also don't see how you could be guaranteed your fair return. What could you do if someone decided not to honor the contract?"

"I suppose it depends on how badly Wen wants to stay in the melon business," I said. "Of course, I'd never give him a lot to begin with. Small amounts first."

Ms. Cao fixed me with an exasperated look. "Are you always scheming like this?"

"Well, I do hate to pass up a chance to make money."

"You're already paid fabulously here," she said. "What difference could watermelon profits possibly make to you?"

"I just thought," I said, "maybe I could start something that would benefit some friends of mine, too."

"Oh no you don't!" Ms. Cao held up her hands in protest. "You're not getting me involved in this!"

"Why not?" I said. "Let me hire you. I obviously can't deal with the Chinese in Chinese. They could run circles around me. In fact, for a reasonable profit, I'd just as soon let it be your business."

"No work, no pay," Ms. Cao said. "Mayflower Compact, remember?"

"I think that was 'no work, no eat.'"

"Whatever."

"But it's my *capital*," I said.

"Yes, but we could pay you back," she said, "and then throw you out."

"As long as I make a reasonable amount on my investment," I said, "that's exactly what I'd like you to do."

"Really? You'd let us take it over?"

"Of course," I said. "I'm not going to be here forever."

"But what I want to know," Ms. Cao said, "is where Wen gets his melons. He *is* Mongolian, so it is possible that he has relatives in the west who have surplus melons to sell. If so, I think I could be persuaded to manage this tiny enterprise. Just the three of us, and the sellers, and some few vendors. My *husband* could even sell melons."

"You could run this business out of your hip pocket," I said.

"That's a new expression on me," Ms. Cao said. She adjusted her glasses. "'Out of your hip pocket.' It must mean 'quite casually.'"

"You're quite hip," I said, "and you'll pocket the profits."

"That's awful." Ms. Cao grinned in spite of herself. "I'm not signing any contract yet. Let's see whether Wen is for real or just full of hot air."

I congratulated Ms. Cao on her nice run of colloquialisms. And so we questioned Wen Da-xing. No, we *grilled* Wen Da-xing. He swore up and down that his connection to the melons was indeed through family members disgruntled with the current rates being paid to them by the Shanghai merchants they had contracted to deal with. According to Wen, the farmers had reasoned quite correctly that they could sell the melons for the same price in Beijing and save considerably on shipping charges.

"Now wait a minute," I said. "How many melons are we talking here?"

Through Ms. Cao, Wen replied, in effect, not very many right now, because the farmers had to honor their contracts with the Shanghai merchants, and these accounted for nearly all the melons available.

"Suppose we bought out the contract from one of the Shanghai guys," I said.

Ms. Cao and Wen were astounded at this notion. They demanded an explanation.

"Suppose I pay the guy what he expects to make selling melons, and take over his contract? Maybe I think I can do the job better, run a more efficient operation, pay him his expected profit, take the melons off his hands, and still make money?"

"He won't want to disappoint his own customers," Ms. Cao said. "He is responsible to many workers, too. It is a terrible idea!"

"Answer my question anyway," I said. "If we had a regular contract for melons, how many tons are we talking about?"

Wen shrugged in dismay and disbelief at this train of thought. Clearly he thought me mad. He said something to Ms. Cao which she translated as "a couple of trainloads, maybe. Fifteen, twenty gondolas full of melons. He doesn't really know."

"If you want to get rich, you've got to think big," I said.

"We don't want to be too rich," Ms. Cao said. "We think too rich is bad. People will despise us."

"We're talking melons," I said, "not Silkworm missiles. This is Beijing, not Hong Kong. How rich do you think we can get? I don't think it is too rich to worry about. Just rich enough to change your life."

Ms. Cao visibly gasped at this idea. She did not translate it for Mr. Wen.

"I believe," she said, "we should begin with a few hundred melons and proceed cautiously. We can inquire about selling more when we are sure we can sell more."

"Excellent," I said. I made an immediate investment in the company of 1,000 *kuai,* an amount nearly equal to three months' salary for Mr. Wen. I also promised to do whatever was necessary in the way of work to get the business on its feet.

As you know, comrades, this entailed sacrificing my taxi ride to work on occasion, with the consequences also of becoming the devoted admirer and business partner of Tai Hai-yan. Fate weaves a tangled web. For if I had not met Tai Hai-yan, or if she had not been so beautiful, say, and a host of other "if... nots", if Chen Tai-pan were still alive! I would not be in your velvet prison writing this confession, fearing for my life.

Fledglings as we were in the melon business, problems accrued. Where, for example, could we sell the melons? Where, when we were oversupplied for a day or two, could we store the excess? (You can imagine how impossible it would be to leave them in the taxi). How could we deal with the complaints and suspicions of other melon dealers anxious to have a share in the limited supply of "surplus" melons? At those times when the three of us were too busy with our regular work unit assignments (not to mention the bicycle business), who, if anyone, could be trusted to take over the melon enterprise?

And this, comrades, is where Chen Tai-pan comes in. He was to become to the watermelon trade what Mr. Whiz was to the bicycle business. I think Chen was the most cultured, and yet the most unassuming man I ever met. And it was by another odd chance that I met him at all. Isn't this the kind of thing, precisely, that makes me love life when I love it, and hate it when I don't?

Mr. Chen had learned to play piano, along with several Chinese instruments, but his daily work was in the city government of Beijing as a kind of supervisor of new construction. He had a positively ass-busting job, no question about it, and yet he never, in my presence at least, showed any signs of being under immense stress, seemed even to delight in snafus and operational disorders (what in the west we would call "disasters" on the job).

Once a week, Mr. Chen was taking lessons from Mr. Ozaku, our Japanese friend from the UNB. In the course of their acquaintance, Mr. Ozaku, himself a great music buff, learned of Mr. Chen's musical interests and prowess, and invited him to hear Beethoven's *Ode to Joy* on a real Japanese stereo system. (As you know, comrades, the popularity of this piece of music in Japan was at the time so immense that the Mitsubishi trucks delivered here had a back-up warning alarm that chimed the melody. I first heard this with my own ears when such a truck was earnestly backing into me and my bicycle — appropriately enough — near the Beijing Hospital. To be crushed by a truck intoning *Ode to Joy*, comrades, is probably a better fate than I deserve, but thankfully the brakes were as good as the music is beloved.) Being also a statesman and a fellow who loved to give surprises, Mr. Ozaku invited several UNB members to this musical event (first, the Boston Symphony version, then the rendition of more than 10,000 Japanese citizens who had gathered in a sports arena to sing this anthem together — really! — the modern world!) which he preceded with a very, very tasteful — the modern world being what it is — Cuban dinner.

Mr. Chen was a delightful, earnest man without any trace of the cynicism you expect to be endemic to his line of work. He spoke Russian, English, French, and was now at age fifty-five, learning some Japanese, and this accomplishment he regarded as routine. He was embarrassed to acknowledge his musicianship when Mr. Ozaku reported it, but denied any great merit in his abilities, lamenting meanwhile that it was difficult for him to find a piano to practice on.

The UNB — God bless them — for once rose to the occasion. Why, Edith said, there was a perfectly good piano going to waste in a storeroom

Riding a Tiger 53

in the Experts' Club. Her daughter had stumbled upon it trying to locate some volleyball stanchions and had just about taken it over as her private instrument. As far as Edith knew, nobody else came near it. Surely, she surmised, Mr. Chen could "inspect" the Experts' Club now and then and spend a pleasant hour or two with the old upright?

Yes, we insisted, we felt the Experts' Club needed almost daily inspection. Who knew when the foundation might crumble?

Mr. Chen responded to the Beijing Beer and the good will with dignity but also with apparent delight.

Naturally, comrades, none of us could resist hearing what Mr. Chen could do with a piano, and when we learned that he was making Tuesdays and Thursdays the evenings for his practice we began slinking around there on the excuse of a card game and became his private audience and fan club. At least Mr. Ozaku and I were among the faithful. Others might come and go, but the two of us were there together at least once a week, and one result was that Ozaku — God damn him! — learned to become a pretty good gin player, at my expense. And after his practice — recital perhaps is a more honest word for it — Mr. Chen would enjoy sharing a bottle of Beijing Beer with us, complaining, comrades, to our alarm, that it was only at restaurants catering to foreigners where this fine beer could be purchased. Since we experts could obtain this beer over the counter at our cafeteria, we promised to bring him a ration to take home every week. It was the least possible payment for his splendid performances.

Having access to a piano and a ready supply of Beijing Beer, Mr. Chen confessed, was very close to happiness. If only his grandchildren could be so blessed!

I think it is fair to say, comrades, that Chen Tai-pan and I became close friends. I was at first quite jealous of his class — behavior, I mean, not origins, which I believe were laboring and mercantile — his humility about his accomplishments and poise. I would think, to be where he is at his age, I would have to learn four languages and six instruments in ten years. Not that I was completely humbled by his presence. I am just vain enough to account my computer knowledge a rough equivalent of his engineering expertise.

And isn't it odd how someone with all of Mr. Chen's talents will be the one who ends up asking the most questions of everyone around? Including me? Mr. Chen queried me endlessly about computers in the course of our conversations, and seemed especially interested in the systems and programs which allow a computer to simulate the sounds of an entire orchestra in a unit no bigger than a bread box. Mr. Ozaku had alerted him that Japanese composers were using computers and that Japanese companies were producing keyboard instruments with memories for rhythms and chords and a wide range of voicings. Fortunately, I could fill him in on some of the details from computer magazines which had come across my desk in recent months. Mr. Chen was awestruck with these developments and their possibilities. He loved the idea that music could be made from simple things — bamboo tubes drilled or lashed together, strings tightened along carved branches, dried animal skins — or from any of the discards of civilization, from oil drums to automobile parts. But he also loved the idea that art and science could be married at the highest levels of technology, too.

"To conceive of such a thing!" he exclaimed. "Just to make music! It's wonderful."

One night I walked him to the bus stop outside the hotel, and he talked at length about how he realized the need for science in China's education and redevelopment, but hoped that it would not overshadow and stunt any longer its enormous artistic heritage and potential. The Cultural Revolution, he confided, had done quite enough to bury culture. He was pleased to see China spending the time and the money to renovate its ancient temples and historical artifacts, to celebrate the sacrifices of the working men, the craftspeople who had realized such wonderful visions.

I told him about the Mitsubishi trucks playing *Ode to Joy* on their backup alarms.

"The Japanese!" he said, stopping in his tracks, then shaking his head, "they are too damned clever. Such a combination is almost an insult, like using Mozart to sell panty hose."

"Mozart might approve," I said, "what little I know of Mozart."

"But still. . . ."

"Of course I see what you mean," I said.

Delighted as I was by his company, I asked if he would join me at the Art Museum that Saturday, to view an exhibit of some contemporary Chinese painters who used classical brush techniques to create contemporary images. I blundered into this invitation even though I had already arranged to meet Tai Hai-yan at the museum, one of the rituals of our romance. Oh well, I thought, what harm can it do for the two of them to meet?

And so we met that next Saturday, and put our noses to paintings, and tried to be civil about what we felt and thought.

"Too many ideas," Chen said, "not enough heart."

"Really?" Tai Hai-yan was offended. "I thought they were quite moving!"

"I know, I know," Chen said. "I am old-fashioned in my tastes. And after seeing these paintings, I yearn so much for some color and some poetry."

"Perhaps it is not so colorful, not so poetic time," Tai Hai-yan said.

"Perhaps not," Chen agreed. He smiled at Tai Hai-yan, and then gave me a look of surprise and appreciation. "Her English is fair," he said, "but her mind is superb. Where did you find her?"

Poor Tai Hai-yan blushed to her roots. She was perfectly unnerved, and could hardly find anything to say after that. What can be harder than to be young and sensitive and bright?

One thing: to be old and sensitive and bright.

Comrades! The friendship of these two people was to be one of the most gratifying I have ever witnessed in my life. To my mind, they were the progressive people of China, each from their separate generations, expecting the best of everything and everyone. Which is to say, they both had unbending faith in the Chinese people, and do not believe their ideals absurd. Their view is not shared by everyone, as you know, including many in power.

The people are in power, Mr. Fisher, and they believe in themselves.

Is this what I am supposed to say? I was merely thinking of some of the cadres, you see.

Do you know a great number of cadres that you can make such judgments?

No, of course not. I knew Chen, of course....

And did he tell you that most cadres were cynical?

No! He said *some* were cynical. Oh, what harm can it do to say as much as he did, since he is dead, and cannot be punished for it? Comrades, he was quite distressed at the degree of cynicism. He believed that you cannot communicate *zeal*, if you are cynical, but can only rule by force and fear. He did not want China to become a country of force and fear. He loves the people too much!

How was he helpful to you in the watermelon trade? You tell us everything but the essentials!

All of this is essential, comrades.

Hats, beer, bicycles, pianos, watermelons — so far you are long on the trivial and short on principles or pertinent facts. You realize, don't you? that this "confession" is turning into a self-serving tome?

Tell me what I should do, then. You seem to have some preconceived idea of what you want. Tell me!
We expect you to recognize your errors, discuss them briefly, and recant.
I'm being as honest as I can be.
How, then, did Chen Tai-pan help you in the watermelon business?
Comrades! Chen Tai-pan was helpful to us in the following ways:
a) He found us good locations for selling watermelons *and* bicycles;
b) he introduced us to people who were willing to abet our unofficial enterprises, and who helped us to expand;
c) he helped us find storage areas;
d) inadvertently, I think, he brought us into contact, and conflict with other unofficial economic institutions, namely the Xinjiang money-changers, a thoroughly bad lot in my view, and perhaps Chen's killers!
Yes?
I believe I have answered your question, comrades.
What you have told us raises more questions than it answers!
Really? Comrades, what did you expect?
You will continue.
Ching nimen gei wo yi ping, lian ping Beijing Pijiu ma?
Yes, comrade Sun will bring some Beijing Beer with your dinner. And now?
And now, comrades, a civilized old Chinese custom which you are trying to eradicate: a nap.

6

COMRADES!
Tonight I am wondering if you are aware that I am "a child of the sixties", as it has been phrased? This is not entirely accurate since I am just a bit too old to have been drafted during the Vietnam war — skirted it several times, enjoying, but not consciously taking advantage of, exemptions for college enrollment and marriage.

For these reasons I was never forced to test my convictions about the stupidity of our government's foreign policy, or the illegality, immorality and undesirability of fighting that war by having the choice thrust upon me to burn my draft card or flee to Canada or enter the service and take my chances. This bit of luck allowed me to continue smug in the belief that the Nuremberg trials had set an enormously important precedent — that the individual was responsible for the actions of the state, had the choice to resist evil and could affect the morality of his government. Just say "No". As much as I still believe that people lead the leaders (except by default, which is most of the time) I no longer feel that everyone can recognize an evil act as it unfolds or that the individual very often has any power to influence the state at all. Public passion is an enormously dangerous thing and institutions themselves impose a psychology that is often determining. A global perspective is learned, not given. Meanwhile, we all suffer a certain degree of programming. We can override this, and yet there are times when we can't, we're trapped in our routines and reformatting is painful. Garbage in, garbage out. You follow me?

This is my confession, then, that I no longer believe that people are free — they are only comparatively free. This relieves us of total responsibility. It preserves, to a limited degree, our victim-hood, or our luckiness. Here's a terrible corollary: some people, in fact, do know better than others. The argument, in politics and in personal life both, is always who knows better? Even in America, land of the Free, enormous energies are in place to regulate pleasure, and other states of mind, through legislation regarding drugs and sex, sometimes even what you can listen to and read and watch. This is considered — as you consider it — legitimate government business. The government presumes to know better.

Interesting, isn't it, that in the sixties when the government was defied for one thing, it was defied for many things? "What is revolution," asketh the playwright, "without general copulation?" A protest musical of the time not only decried the war but celebrated fellatio and cunnilingus, sex crimes in many states. Interesting to note, too, that in an attempt to restore and gain prerogatives, the government emphasizes regulating our personal morality and personal states of mind. "Say 'No' until otherwise instructed": this is the perfect formula for public order.

But what is the rationale? The stated rationale, comrades, is that these activities are a threat to our society. But I see no apparent threat to society in fellatio, for example. As for drugs, I know that they can be used harmlessly, but not by everyone, and that they do create economic emergencies for those who become addicted. What's the threat? The drugs themselves? The economic emergency? The addiction? Tell us about opium, comrades. In a medical context, it is as innocent as a gun, and I wonder if the overall harm to society is any greater than that caused by automobiles, cigarettes, or hot dogs. You apparently think so, for your technique of dealing with dealers is ultimately straightforward: a bullet to the back of the head, and no trial. There are people in American neighborhoods where drug lords have muscled into their everyday lives who would agree with this method. And yet they have not had China's history of being exploited by drugs, and by addiction. Many of them, if not most, do not even know the difference between drugs which cause addiction and those which do not. In large measure, the laws themselves create the criminals. What, after all, are we being protected from? From unofficial forms of pleasure, and from unofficial states of mind?

Consider, are drugs more dangerous to us than the nuclear weapons which the government hoards and does so little to remove from our future? And what is the relation between the failure of government to remove fear from our lives and the dependence on drugs? There is a degree of hypocrisy in all this. The government may know better, but it is not truly our safety that motivates it! And a government that lies about its reasons either doesn't really know better after all, or knows only too well the truth and is afraid of unleashing that public passion against itself. Hence also, the great utility of enemies, to focus that passion outwards. Nothing preserves tyranny like the perceived threat of an invasion. Little Nicaragua, three million strong, half of these under fifteen years old, is a threat to America! (Why, then, we had better fear Rhode Island, too, with double the population). And Russia serves as a beacon for both your nation and mine. Very handy! The US itself, of course, is on every tyrant's hit list, and is fast becoming the world's most popular scapegoat. We bad. Them outside agitators, you know, them wants our wimmens, our refrigerators, our *jao zi*. Our blue jeans. Our watermelons. Our jade, silk, tea. Our minds and strong backs. Our — excuse me, comrades, — tits and asses, too. Our money at the most favorable exchange rates. Our problems, our troubles, our diseases, our anxieties, our misconceptions, our historical tragedies: no one wants these, although, comrades, I believe a very good buck is to be made — is made daily — on just these things.

Consider American fat, which disgusts so many Chinese. Comrades! There's billions in it! I would give anything to be slimmer, to be as sleek as Ms. Cao, say, or even comrade Sun, who has just opened the door to make sure I am writing and not otherwise indulging myself. Satisfied, he smiles and ducks out again. Consider slim-down camps for Americans, comrades, a healthy Chinese diet, bicycle riding, digging in the communal garden, *tai chi* lessons. Believe me, there are Westerners who would pay for this. And the reason? Fat! Fat, and vanity.

So, comrades, this almost child of the sixties (spawn of farmers and factory workers, mental heir of populism and beatniks) became a warrior for peace on the home front — the contradictions of no significance, except to create some energy by their very friction. Already I was interested in computers, unaware that they would change my life, even bring me to China.

You see how interconnected these things are? I thought it hideous that the military had become so computerized, that guns were fired and aimed by computer control, that lead and fire saturated the Vietnamese air according to the computerized formulas of "overkill". There was no room left for the soldier in such a technocratic war and morale problems among the troops were not the fault of public dissension alone. The first television war was also the first computerized war and when computers are making decisions the role of the soldier is that of the robot — which may literally become the fate of soldiers someday soon. "Be all you can be" our advertisements for the Army sing: meaning just what it says and not what it implies. But the idea of becoming a robot doesn't sell.

You must also not imagine that I am naive about how you may choose to use the computer expertise I have been sharing with you here. The computer is like everything in this life, like guns, or drugs, or sex: they can be used and abused, can bring us together or blow us apart. Very few things retain their innocence and integrity when a human being lays hands on them. This is a problem for science, facts wobble depending on who touches them. I know very well, for example, that Silkworm missiles are not guided by Chinese midgets with tiny steering wheels in their hands. Computers are involved and there is nothing to say, no matter what my wishes may be, that some of the expertise I have passed along here may not some day come roaring back at soldiers of my own country out on the Persian Gulf or over some frozen and dismal Korean terrain. In cases like this, today, it is literally impossible to assess the degree of one's guilt. All we can say for sure is that we are probably never innocent.

Silkworm missiles. Funny, I always associated silk with a luxurious and peaceful world, with cool shirts on a summer day, with dresses that so nicely hug the female form. In my country we have something called the Peacemaker, a thermonuclear device which could turn Manchuria to glass and take a big, big bite out of the world's future. At least you ban George Orwell. You make no bones about appropriating double-think and double-speak when it comes to military things. In America we just depend on public ignorance.

Myself, I never protested the soldier, because I had no proof of my own that, had my luck been different, I would have resisted, would not have "gone along with the program". I never blamed a soldier for being where he was, doing what he was doing, but I blamed the government for putting him there. I objected strongly to anyone who blamed the soldier, which was like blaming the symptom for the disease — and besides that, many who blamed the soldier were never themselves imperiled either by the draft or by the terrible necessities of combat, the sometimes grotesque necessities of survival in a nightmarishly unconventional war. Forget honor. Forget patriotism. Forget orders. The main job was to stay alive. Among other things, that war was a total assault on the dignity of the soldier, and what soldiering has historically meant. The veterans did not need any more grief from the community when they returned — but they frequently got it anyway. This enraged me.

But my own passions had been stirred, comrades. I was not above the historical moment. And on the campus where I happened to be teaching there also happened to be a large ROTC — Reserve Officers' Training Corps — program with its own building. I never understood what relation ROTC (the students pronounced it "Rotsy", suggesting their disgust) had with education, but then again I know that religious officers are trotted out to say prayers at every public function and that every professional game begins with the national anthem and that this mixing-up of authoritarian symbols in our daily life goes on constantly. It was only the war, however, that made me realize my campus was contributing materially to the war effort by supplying trained military personnel — badly trained, some said, but that didn't matter to me.

Mind you, I did not stop paying taxes, even though I knew (and know) very well that about 50 per cent of them, almost 12.5 per cent of my entire salary, was going for military purposes. This aggravates me now as it did then, but I have the same lack of gumption, of nerve, to just say no. Saying no would probably land me in jail. (Consider that, comrades! *Me!* In jail!) I'm free to say no insofar as I'm willing to sacrifice my freedom in the land of the Free. Let's have no illusions about who's in charge, about the freedom, existential or otherwise, of the individual. I'm sure we agree on this point. How long have I been in this room now? Almost two weeks? I don't feel sorry for myself. I am not Nelson Mandela.

Nevertheless, impassioned as I was, morally certain as I was, I decided on what I regarded as a revolutionary action. Over the course of several weeks I filled a dozen or so one-gallon cider jars with gasoline and stored these in a locked closet in my garage. (As for the interconnectedness of things: the cider jars were linked to ideas of my wife and our housemates about the virtues of a sugar-free existence. Now *that* I won't go into now, except to note how wonderfully thin I was back then. And how unhappy!) I also visited the ROTC building several times and got a pretty good idea of its layout. Young as I was, I still had a professorial air, and nobody stopped me, or questioned me. The one precaution I took was to carry a clipboard filled with papers, on the advice of a thief I had met in Chicago — another story I'll pass over here. Wear a hard-hat and a tie and carry a clipboard, the thief said, and you can go almost anywhere.

The ROTC building was the campus's oldest, and I supposed that with its grand central staircase running from the first to the third floors, we had here a natural 'chimney' that would allow fire to spread quickly throughout the whole edifice. I also noted other strategic locations such as the weapons storeroom and the administrative and record-keeping area and even a small room in the attic where, legend had it, an FBI (Federal Bureau of Investigation) transmitter had been lodged. I was going to do this all in. I figured it would take me half an hour to set it up, and in another hour the building would be a blazing shell.

Comrades! I told absolutely no one about this venture. I trusted friends, but I did not trust them to keep such a secret forever. And I certainly did not trust any organization I belonged to then to be free of informants or agitators. No one could claim responsibility for the act I was about to perform, and yet it would be everyone's victory.

I think the night I was compelled to act was the night that I, along with millions of other Americans, saw on television a Viet Cong suspect executed by a point-blank shot to the temple. My young wife and I were at the time living with another couple and sharing the raising and nurturing of our children, a kind of compromise commune. We spent the evening raging over the war. (My daughter was to grow up believing "Nix-on" was a dragon! She asked me one night as I tucked her into bed "is Nix-on coming to get us?" I almost wept. How early our innocence is trampled! Even I remember sitting at the family breakfast table, preschool age, watching my father and mother draw lines on a map showing the progress of the Allies against the Nazis in Europe. I could not have understood the details, but they communicated the intensity of their concern, and I knew there was something evil in the air, some terrible thing happening in a world I could not see. My own daughter was to grow up in a similarly corrupt air.) That night, very late, in the darkness of our garage, I loaded twelve gallons of "Apple Cider" into the trunk of my car and put two boxes of kitchen matches in my jacket pocket and set out to destroy the cancer of the ROTC building on our little Midwestern campus.

Innocent America! Native son with a carload of gasoline in bottles. The campus snoozed. The security cop was down at the gym checking locks on the towel bins. The janitors had long since drifted home. I unloaded my three boxes by a basement window, kicked out all the panes, and let myself in, then hauled the boxes in after me. I used my flashlight as sparingly as possible, and I started at the top, placing and tipping over bottles as I moved along, of course maintaining a continuous stream of gasoline, and intermittently leaving a little mound of matches to spur the flaming dragon along.

The smell was tremendous, almost more than I could bear, but my fervor was next to perfect. My heart pounded like a fire alarm, and my hands were sweaty inside the little cotton gloves. Of course my head filled with every terrible fantasy: how the door would fly open and a cop with a lighted cigar would step in; how the spark from a motor turning on would blow the building before I was out of it; how an innocent person, a janitor, say, would be roasted in the blaze. I kept my nerve pretty well, however, and quite quickly had the dozen bottles in place, tipped, gurgling, the building itself oozing gasoline and charged with vapors.

I stood by the window in the basement surrounded by white dishes, as I recall, in what must have been the store room of the mess. I took out the remaining box of matches and before I lit one, made sure of my escape route, over a table and back out through the window. All I had to do now was light a match, and the flames would trail out through the doorway and into the main stairwell of the evil ROTC building and WHOOM! A victory for the People!

All I had to do was light a match, comrades! That's all! In fact, I thought I had better light a match at this point because surely I had left footprints or other evidence and I was sure to be discovered as the perpetrator if the fire did not consume all those tell-tale bits of body oil and hair and fiber, all those little marks we inevitably leave behind, like any animal.

A match, a match, a match. There was the match, there was the box with its abrasive surface, clamoring for a spark.

I went home, I showered, I woke my wife and made love to her. I lay awake hoping to hear clamor, sirens.

I learned something. Perhaps I was a coward. But not only could I not take a human life, I could not even destroy a building! Mere property! I realized I was utterly useless as a revolutionary. What would Sam Adams, Thomas Paine, Denmark Vesey have thought of me? As much as I hated the military and its tactics, I could never become one of them. I could not pull a trigger, could not light a match.

What happened?

I don't understand.

The building full of gasoline. Did it burn down?

No. No, no. The local fire department called in a special unit from a big city airport and the building was flooded with a gasoline-absorbing foam. In the process, of course, every trace I might have left behind was scrubbed and washed away. At least the building was shut down for a while, and the action got national press. There was also a serious investigation that sent every leftist organization in the area diving for cover. ROTC began posting guards at the building and the college's administrative offices were given round-the-clock observation and so a certain institutional innocence was lost. I regret that. I think you ought to be able to leave your car, and your house unlocked and I don't think you're to blame if you fail to do these things and someone rips you off. Anyway, local gossip was tremendous about who could have done it. I was utterly miserable.

Why was that?

I just told you! The whole purpose of telling the story was to confess my incapacity to take a revolutionary action. I'm not a violent person. In other words, I'm dangerous to no one — a way of saying, possibly, "impotent".

But surely you agree that ideas can be dangerous. Isn't the pen mightier than the sword?

If it saves my neck, I might believe it. But the pen does not always work for good, as the maxim implies. We know the power of propaganda, certainly, and the willingness of certain people to whore for ideology. This will require no explanation, surely.

Are you suggesting propagandists are whores?

Comrades, please! I am not a writer. You can't hold me responsible for every silly thing I say?

You have just said that the pen can be as evil as the gun.

Why is this confession of mine so important to you?

You feel you are being used.

I suspect it, yes.

Mr. Fisher, your confession is for your own good. Believe this, and all will be well. Believe this, and continue.

For my own good. Sure.

7

I DON'T KNOW WHAT IT'S LIKE out there in the grasslands, know next to nothing about Mongolia. After eighteen months in China, I still can't be sure that I can tell the difference between Mongol and Han any more than I can with certainty tell the difference between a Korean and Japanese. No more would I expect you to distinguish between an Australian and a Canadian by sight alone, or tell Frenchman from Spaniard, Berber from Jew, Ibo from Dahomian. There are differences, to be sure, but it takes considerable experience to make such distinctions readily and accurately, and who among us is so worldly? I presume God Himself is sometimes confused and shakes the divine head with dismay at the rationales for our endless wars. You materialist rascals! We superstitious dupes! Our God and our Flag are our immortality. Bite the dust, infidel! We die with honor, you die with shame.

It is hard to imagine a place like Mongolia in the thermonuclear age — a land of cowboys and horsemen and tribal customs. Surrounded by Russia with narrow doors open to the Moslem world, well-trodden paths to war-sick realms. Camels once bedded down at the gates to the Forbidden City! You can see turbans galore in Xian, even a great mosque where the words of Mohammed are piped through loudspeakers and heard, but not understood, by German tourists looking for bargains in the nearby streets.

Sometimes geography is bunk, comrades, by which I mean identities are never as definite as boundaries. As Texas is Mexican, so Mongolia is Russian, Afghani, Pakistani, one image stamped on another. The Kurds? The Meo? Boundaries are nothing to them but nuisances. They cross borders like clouds. And human boundaries always blur. Besides war, the one thing the world will always know is Midnight Integration. I myself, I might have had children with yellow skin!

Comrades! I am taking the epic approach tonight because it became apparent to me in the course of events that our little, unofficial enterprise of selling watermelons was becoming entangled in a web of outlaw associations that spanned the city, the nation, and the globe. There is clearly no such thing as an international watermelon conspiracy, but you know very well that drug trafficking is international, and so, apparently, is money-changing. Yes! There are people who will kill to get their hands on Japanese *yen*, or all else failing, even American dollars.

Now in China one of the connecting routes to the world's mischief leads through Hong Kong, as everyone knows. The comparative demise of free ports like Tangiers (I mourn its passing!) has allowed Hong Kong to become a beacon unto outlaws everywhere, a haven for the ruthless and freewheeling, like pirate ports of yesteryear. But the old Silk Road, comrades, is not innocent either. China is a wonderful country, freer of corruption than most, but, comrades, you cannot claim to be pure. There is a little outlaw blood in all of us. Thank God!

Now Chen Tai-pan, as I began to relate, in his role as construction supervisor and city building inspector, was able to find us several locations where we could sell our melons, if and when we had melons. At first we rotated our sales through these sites, so as not to be too easily pinned down, rather like a floating crap game. And never mind where we heaped our melons, the public found us, bartered, paid. Poor Wen, the taxi driver, working all day and half the night — he was beginning to look downright haggard.

What we also realized in the course of business was that if we had enough melons, we could sell them at each and every one of the locations Chen found for us. In the giddiness of our profit making, Ms. Cao, Wen Da-xing and I sometimes sighed, "Alas, we cannot get more produce!" Soon enough, however, our horizons were to broaden, but before I get into that — which will also explain my epic approach to this portion of my self-criticism — I want to dispense with a question, if I can, comrades, that I know is burning in your hearts.

Why, you must be asking, would a cultured, well-placed, apparently serene man like Chen Tai-pan ever involve himself, dirty his hands, shall we say, in such a petty criminal business as watermelon trafficking?

I have asked myself this question many times, and one answer is also the non-answer: Chen Tai-pan was, after all, a very complex individual, whose motives were beyond my limited ability to fathom. Once I thought he was doing it mainly out of friendship, but it became apparent also, comrades, that he enjoyed the business and was curious to death — I speak too truly! — about its progress. He took only a minute portion of the profits to begin with, but he also reinvested *everything* coming to him. Everything! I don't believe he even sported himself to a banquet.

I know he liked the fact that we were dealing here with a wholesome product and that all of us in the business were otherwise honest and hardworking people. Perhaps that seems strange in your eyes, comrades, that we should regard ourselves as saintly when clearly operating in violation of so many regulations and so many principles.

Oh, I don't know! It also seemed to me that running a quasi-legal business seemed to strike some profound chord in Chen, as if it were in his very genes to wheel and deal. Only a genius, I think, could have kept from smothering in his official job, one aggravating detail, argument, and mix-up after another. Maybe, in part, the watermelon business was an antidote to that. Still, I insist that maybe it was all just in the cultural genes. You Chinese know how to, you love to bargain and barter, buy and sell. Don't tell me I am stereotyping! Once in China no one was deemed more lowly than the merchant, but someone forgot to tell the merchants that, and many a great Mandarin household was supported by the marketplace. You appreciate, and can recognize excellence. You appreciate all things, from watermelons and beer, to books and opera! I see the state store with its fixed prices almost bare of customers while the free market across the street is thronged, bubbling with debate. I am not blind. And so I think Chen was, in a way, acting on this cultural legacy.

But most of all, comrades, I think Chen Tai-pan's fatal flaw, like that of Ms. Cao and Wen Da-xing, and, yes, even me, was impatience. All of us were united in wanting, as soon as possible, what we imagined to be a richer life — and not just better television programs. (America is no model for the world, by the way, on that score!) What I saw in Chen, Wen and Cao — even in Tai Hai-yan — was a desire for some personal space, and more variety in what they could do, and learn to do. As much as anything I think they were fighting tedium and stagnation, seeking adventure and growth.

To return to the topic at hand, *viz.,* the expansion of the watermelon business. Having now several sales locations and storage places available to us, we all lamented not having the melons to load them with. A few of these locations, naturally, became temporary bicycle sales centers, but in that business our rate of production could never keep pace with demand anyway and sales space was not much of a problem. What Mr. Whiz fixed we had someone waiting for. Tai Hai-yan had a notebook filled with the names of eager buyers. Check that notebook, comrades, and you will find many interesting names, I'm sure, perhaps a few you recognize. Look at N° 113, for example, Wu Ko-chu. The little ingrate! The little romantic! The little squealer! He's the one who tipped the first domino. What an odd lottery this life can be. And damn the luck! That he should imagine himself in love with Tai Hai-yan! He hardly even knew her. The thought of it — N° 113 no less — still irks me profoundly.

About this time, when we were ripe — pardon me — Mr. Wen, our taxi driver with the connections to the watermelon producing relatives, informed us we *could* purchase more melons *if* we could pay for them in FEC (Foreign Exchange Certificates) or American dollars. Was this a coincidence, comrades? Or had Wen been waiting all along for the right moment to pounce with this news?

This put the burden squarely on my shoulders. I was quite aware, as any *weiguoren* or tourist has to be in Beijing, that there was an active black market for foreign currency and that on almost any street corner in certain neighborhoods you could get five or five and a half *renminbi* for a US buck as against the 3.7 official exchange rate. My mistake was that I had assumed this was a local enterprise and that the American cash and FEC were used by Beijingers to purchase those specialty goods in Friendship Stores that were otherwise severely rationed or downright forbidden to Chinese citizens. I mean, it was instantly apparent to me from the crowds in every Chinese department store that Beijingers have a healthy appetite for consumer goods and are frustrated by both limited supply and limited income. When I was approached on the street by the money-changers, my only thought was Aha! This is how some people manage to buy that Japanese boom box or camera, that black leather jacket or bottle of French cologne. Pity the tourists, I thought, who fall for this game, and then discover they cannot — legally, at least — spend the Peoples' Republic currency! The "white card" I had, as you know, comrades, allowed me to spend Chinese money, but I never, in the normal course of my life, dealt with the money-changers on the corner. I didn't trust them. They were, it seemed to me, too punkish, too insistent, and my response to their impolite and dogged entreaties was to grow stubborn. They were hard sell guys. I said "nuts!"

Therefore, my initial response to Wen's news that we could get more melons through foreign dollars was to ask why this should be the case, why Chinese money wasn't "good enough" for them. Could that many farmers, I wondered, want that many televisions? I could get the US dollars, no problem. That was part of my contract, that I could take up to fifty per cent of my pay in US cash and/or FEC. Besides, I had a hidden stash of US currency that I kept for an emergency, in case I had to fly home or have special medical attention in Tokyo or Hong Kong, etc., etc. So it wasn't a question of hassling around for the foreign bucks. I just wanted to know the scoop.

Wen declined to offer the details while Ms. Cao was present, but one afternoon when I was alone in the cab with him (and about fifty melons in the back seat and trunk, giving the cab a wonderful, sweet aroma and a brutal bounce on its overburdened shock absorbers) he was more forthcoming.

"Money-changers," he said, "mostly Mongolians. Like my relatives, all come from west China. Old Silk Road. Right?"

"Right."

"They change money, then use money two ways. First, set up shop. Usually clothes. Sell clothes to tourists, get more FEC, dollars, *yen*. Two," he held up his fingers in a way I thought might have been a little parody of my own way of speaking and gesturing, "use foreign currency to buy...."

"Don't tell me," I said. "Boom boxes. Televisions. Marlboros."

"No, no." Wen shook his head impatiently. "Japanese motorcycle!"

"*Motor*cycles?" Well, I thought, I should have guessed. I didn't like to think of Beijing changing from "the city of bicycles" to the "city of motorbikes" or of what a thunderous city it would be if people stopped pedaling and started popping along. Still, I supposed, such a future was probably inevitable. God! Think of the smog! And yet it made sense in another way:

"I guess out West there people can ride motorbikes without getting stopped and questioned, with all those wide open spaces?" I said.

"No, no." Again Wen waved me silent. "Chinese no buy motorbike. *Russians* buy."

"What?"

"We buy Japanese motorbikes from Koreans, see? Sell motorbikes to Russians."

"Can't see what good Russian currency would be here," I said.

"No, not for money." Wen sighed. "We sell motorbikes to Russians for Russian *truck*."

"Ah! You *trade* them for Russian trucks."

"Yes, yes!" He was delighted I understood.

"But what in God's name do you want with Russian trucks?"

"Sell to Pakistani."

"Aha. What do the Pakistanis trade for Russian trucks?"

"Some things, I don't know."

I had assumed that somewhere down the trial of these transactions things would begin to grow murky, but I didn't like it, all the same. Did Wen know, or did he not know? "What about drugs?" I asked bluntly. "Or weapons?"

"Drugs too dangerous," Wen said.

"Yes. Pretty serious penalty if you get caught in the drug trade. Most serious!"

Wen shrugged. "China police not too serious."

"Not much," I said. "They catch you with drugs, they kill you. Not serious at all."

"Drug gangs much worse," Wen said. "Rob you, torture you, make you slave. Then kill you. My people," Wen cut the air with an open hand, "no drugs. Drugs for crazy men."

"Well, if you ever find out what the Pakis trade for Russian trucks, you must tell me," I said. "I'll sleep better knowing."

"Maybe," Wen said.

Maybe, right, I thought, remembering momentarily Krazy Kirby's exchange with the British journalist on all the things we really didn't want to know, but should. Such as where our hard-earned money eventually ends up, like raindrops trickling into a river flowing into the sea. Old dollars never die. They just end up in Swiss bank accounts. Not that everything starts with us, or that the *yen* stops here. But we grease some palms and grease some wheels we prefer to forget about, too. Who am I to tell the Pakis what to do with their Russian trucks?

The truth is, at that moment in my criminal education, it all gave me a gratifying sense of community. Bicycles and watermelons seemed pretty small potatoes against this backdrop, and considering world weapons dealings and arms-for-hostages scandals and the like, seemed truly innocent, too. But is anything concerned with profit truly untainted? I am sure that you, comrades, have spent many hours wrestling with this question, and will wrestle with it many more hours before you are through. Oddly enough, it doesn't trouble the sleep of many Americans, I'm sure. You won't find Americans very often chasing their own tails.

So, I coughed up a good chunk of my emergency stash. When I counted the bills into Wen's hands his eyes got larger with every C-note. I kept asking myself why I was doing it, what I thought I could possibly even *do* with all the *renminbi* that would come rolling in as a result of our watermelon sales. Antiques, rugs, silk, I thought. How else was I going to spend my profits? When I returned to the US I was obviously going to have a lot of Chinese gear to sell. Me? In the rug business? I'd much rather sell bikinis — silk bikinis. Meanwhile, I wasn't pressured and had lots of time to plan — this is one of life's little illusions anyway — my *renminbi*-rich future.

Comrades! I'm afraid that I must now confess that although I had paid for a railroad gondola full of melons, I really had no imagination for how much space they would occupy (how many taxi loads), how much they would weigh, or how long it would take to move them. Somehow I just took it for granted that Wen, Cao and I would supervise the off-loading of the melons into trucks that would take them to our sales locations. I had been in China long enough to know better, and how I lulled myself into thinking otherwise I have no idea, and no excuse. Except: I *was* deeply involved also in my work unit duties; the bicycle business required some attention; I enjoyed my evenings with the UNB and listening to Chen Tai-pan practice piano; I did also moon stupidly and relentlessly after the body and companionship of the ever-virgin Tai Hai-yan; and I was getting tremendous pleasure out of being with my colleague and partner in watermelon crime, Cao Song-wen. I suppose, in fact, besides the many distractions, I really didn't believe a gondola full of melons would someday arrive. And also in fact, the first such shipment took so long to appear that I had almost forgotten it was due.

This is how it worked: the day before the gondola was to arrive, Wen informed me that a train carrying melons would appear in the Beijing station at about 10 PM. The gondola carrying our melons — number 707-414-698 — would be shunted to a siding near a high, brick boundary wall between that hour and 1 AM. We would have from 1 AM until 4 AM to unload the car and get out of sight.

True enough, comrades, it was now utterly apparent to me that we had entered into a new realm of activity, one that was not just a little *sub rosa* but *bona fide* illegal. We had to steal our own melons! It was nuts! This being China, however — Beijing anyway — I was not surprised, just annoyed. What was I going to do? Kiss off my thousand bucks? Let a gondola full of melons go to rot and ruin while a city clamored for them? The whole thing gave me a headache, but I knew I was trapped into this for good and aye. Why hadn't I planned ahead? I cursed myself up one side and down the other. I was beginning to learn something every real consumer knows: sometimes a bargain is not really a bargain after all.

Wen gave me another little nudge. We were going to need some help to unload a gondola in a mere three hours, and we were going to need something also besides one taxi to haul them away.

"Jesus Christ!" I exploded. "I'm supposed to be at a meeting of millet growers this evening. I haven't got time to set up a whole midnight off-loading operation, too. Don't you have some strings you can pull?"

Wen allowed as how his connections were already being deployed in getting the gondola to the appointed place near the wall.

What else could I do? Naturally I called Chen Tai-pan, the most resourceful person I knew, and asked if he could possibly, somehow, round up a truck or two to help us transport our watermelon bonanza. He'd look into it, he said. He thought it was possible, and I gave him the location to send the trucks to. He was to let me know only if he could *not* send the trucks and otherwise I could count on them being there. Beyond this, the only people I could ask for their labor were Ms. Cao, who was ready and willing, and my beloved Tai Hai-yan, and Mr. Whiz. This was above and beyond the call of duty, as Mr. Whiz and Hai-yan well understood, but they readily assented anyway, Mr. Whiz for a reasonable wage, Hai-yan for the adventure of it.

If all went well, then, I would have four men (myself, Chen, Wen, and Mr. Whiz) and two women (Ms. Cao and Hai-yan) to unload and transport a gondola full of melons in three hours. I decided to organize the detail in this way, at least until fatigue required a change of roles: Chen, the oldest man, and Wen, the most experienced driver, in the trucks; Mr. Whiz and Ms. Cao, the strongest, first shift in the gondola, unloading; myself and Hai-yan catching the melons and loading the trucks. I assumed I could make adjustments once I saw how the work flow developed, and if a driver could unload quickly between runs, then perhaps I could climb in the gondola, too. I communicated this to all hands, told them to rest as much as possible during the forthcoming day, and the next night, at the appointed hour, all were ready.

If only it had been that simple! In America, we have a law, named Murphy's Law, that states that anything that can go wrong will go wrong, and usually all at once. I'm sure you have a similar rule in China, maybe a Wang's Law or a Zhang's Law that says the same thing. On this night the Murphy/Wang Laws were operating to the fourth power. It's just damned lucky no one was killed.

The first mistake I made was to stop by the café at Building Nº 1 in the You Yi Bing Guan for a Wu Sying bracer or two before setting out on my midnight ramble. At that late hour, the café was teeming with the African contingent mostly, but also there was our Canadian lunatic, Krazy Kirby. For whatever reason, perhaps because I was the only other white face in the joint at that hour, Krazy Kirby latched onto me at once, and I could not get rid of him. This was trying in the extreme, but when I insulted him he only laughed, and if I ignored him, he only seemed more inspired in his manic lecturing. He was the last thing I needed, especially since I wanted a clear mind and steady nerves for the business ahead of me. It was no go, however. Kirby was on me like a Velcro fastener, and when I grabbed a cab for the railroad station, the son-of-a-bitch forced himself in beside me, gabbing away!

Thus I arrived at the destination assigned just after midnight in the company of the You Yi Bing Guan's resident Cassandra. Comrades? How can I communicate to you the immense frustration I felt about this? It was as if someone had, in the manner of the antique Chinese punishment of villains, tied a lead ball around my neck. I had no choice, however, but to greet my associates in the watermelon trade and lay out the operation as I thought it should go, Krazy Kirby's head bobbing over my shoulder, taking everything in with those intense blue eyes.

Now I encountered a second little problem. Chen Tai-pan for all his connections, was unable to supply the trucks (pay attention, comrades! this detail is crucial to subsequent events) but could, on such short notice, procure only one, and also a wagon pulled by a mule. So there the six of us were, with the addition of Krazy Kirby and a mule. As you might expect, we were all quite agitated — except for the mule, who kept nodding off, and Krazy Kirby, who seemed to find the whole event of high and hilarious interest.

Mr. Whiz, Wen and I were helped over the wall by the others and after some searching we located our gondola. This, at least, was well-placed, close to a curve in the wall in a very dark area between streetlights. There was a much larger gap between the gondola and the wall than I had hoped, but the top of the watermelon load was higher than the wall itself. And I must say, comrades, you cannot imagine how my heart raced with both satisfaction and dread when I hauled myself up the rusty ladder attached to the gondola and saw what a huge trove of melons we indeed had before us. Was it five or ten tons of melons? I have no way to judge. It was, in Americanese, a genuine "shitload". It took my breath away. If I had opened a casket to find it filled with jewels, I would have been no less stupefied.

Therefore, with great excitement, we set to work. We decided to load the cart first, which Chen Tai-pan volunteered to drive, offering the brief and cryptic excuse that he had learned the trade during the Cultural Revolution. I mentally made a note of this, telling myself that when we were thrown together in prison, I would ask him about those years. As long as Krazy Kirby was with us, and having already some unfortunate direct experience of his strength, I saw no reason not to send him into the gondola to pitch melons with Mr. Whiz. Ms. Cao and I mounted the wall and found footholds, and the rest of our gang formed a line from the wall to the melons.

"O.K.," I said. "Go!"

Comrades?

I doubt that any of you can appreciate the chaos which followed. You would have thought, to begin with, that Kirby and Mr. Whiz were engaged in Olympic competition, so thick and fast was the rain of melons they began to heap upon us. I find now in recollection, great difficulty in communicating the awesome, frightening sensation of one basketball-sized melon after another hurtling upon you out of the darkness — an exercise a little like trying to catch cannonballs, I think, and something akin, truly, to religious experience. Ms. Cao and I were quickly overwhelmed, and I now know that among the saddest sounds in the world is that of a four or five or eight *kuai* melon splattering on a Beijing sidewalk.

"Whoa! Whoa!" I called, to no avail, since Kirby and Mr. Whiz in their frenzy of labor apparently took this to mean "Go! Go!"

"Stop!" I commanded, and this finally brought results.

We quickly reorganized. I climbed into the gondola and put Kirby on the wall to work with Mr. Whiz, imagining them a more balanced battery. Now I lobbed melons to Ms. Cao, at about one fifth the rate of Mr. Whiz, but this seemed also to bring about a reasonable rate of progress. I labored steadily and earnestly for about, oh, thirty? thirty-five? melons, when it became readily apparent that I would probably die of heart attack or stroke before even a barely noticeable dent in the huge stockpile of melons beneath our feet. Nevertheless, I bent down, grasped the cool, slippery melons, pitched them in a gentle arc to Ms. Cao who curled them into her chest, then dropped them to one of the workers below.

Kirby and Quick-as-Death, as I now thought of him (*"Hen Quai Dao Sui,"* Ms. Cao muttered) were now chanting in rhythm as they tossed and caught and dropped — *Yi Er San Sz, Yi Er San Sz* — and seemed genuinely to be making a game of how rapidly they could work and how much zip they could put on the melons. By contrast, I think I had logged a measly hundred, hundred-twenty melons when I was dizzy enough to collapse. Ms. Cao waved me to a halt, dropped from the wall into the blackness, then emerged at the rim of the gondola.

"Let's trade places for a while," she advised.

I had seen Chinese laborers napping everywhere, at every opportunity, in the most incredible circumstances, including, once, in the bed of a moving truckload of rocks. Suddenly I understood how this was possible. At that moment, I could have laid down in the melons and slept blissfully until dawn! And we were only just beginning. It was all I could do to drag myself up the wall.

From this fresh vantage point I saw that the crew on the street had found it necessary to do some quick thinking of their own and had hired some late night street people to help them pass the melons along and load them on the cart. Compared to the cool quietude of the gondola interior, the street seemed riotous with energy, with the bustle of so many people, the rumble of melons across the boards of the mule cart. Later I learned the deal that had been struck was this: fifteen melons for the company, one for the crew — a staggering 7.5 per cent of our melons just to keep up with the flow provided by Kirby and Mr. Whiz!

Finally, of course, the cart was loaded, and Chen Tai-pan was flicking the whip over the neck of the recalcitrant mule. I gave a silent cheer as he clip-clopped out of sight — silent because I had almost no breath at all.

Now, comrades, I may have said that we also had a truck, but the truth is that what Chen found for us was a Mitsubishi touring mini-bus, capable of holding about a dozen people or, by my estimate, about 600 to 750 melons, 150 to 190 dollars' worth, and only about one-tenth of the melons we had to move in total. I doubt if you have ever seen what a Mitsubishi touring bus looks like when it is loaded to capacity with watermelons, but I assure you it resembles what it would like if filled with water itself — the frame is so loaded down that it rubs on the very wheels, and the bus sways as if at any moment it might simply topple. In my dreamy, fatigued state, it was all too easy to imagine the street splattered with watermelon gore. The bus literally groaned as Wen ambled away, grinding gears, rocking, banging through potholes.

While bus and cart were gone, we nevertheless continued to heave and pile. A moon emerged — what in the American west would be called a "rustler's moon", half full, bright enough to steal melons by, but not so bright as to make you an easy target.

Ms. Cao finally sat down in a swoon of fatigue. I called for Hai-yan to take her place, helped her scale the wall by grasping her lovely hands and yet almost without the strength to pull her up. If anything, this youngster seemed exhilarated, eager for more. When she sat beside me atop the wall, she exclaimed:

"Oh! Still so many melon!"

Already I had sacrificed the notion of emptying the gondola, was steeling myself to get away with what we could, hoping it would at least bring us to the break even point. That is, bring me to that point. All those melons still to be moved! Each one was a note in an opera of folly.

"Let's not kill ourselves," I said. "Let's just get what we can, while we can."

"*Yi Er San Sz,*" Kirby and Mr. Whiz chanted. The melons continued to fly. "*Yi Er San Sz.*"

Unbeknownst to us, the Zhang/Murphy Laws were operating about two blocks away, where a combination of pothole, glass and overload proved fatal to a rear tire on the bus. Wen, as you might guess, was miserable to the point of suicide, since he knew it would be futile to attempt to jack up a bus full of melons which, unlike passengers, could not be ordered to dismount while the repairs took place. Unable to repair the tire and not wanting to be questioned about a bus full of melons, Wen decided *to hell with it* and roared along with the bus at a terrible tilt, scraping the pavement and throwing sparks, the tire flopping and the rim getting pounded hopelessly, relentlessly out of round. When he reached the storage area, owing to the tilt of the bus, Wen had only to open the rear doors and the bus nearly unloaded itself, Wen having little more to do than unjam the melons when they happened to cluster in the doorway.

All the same, the bus was clearly lost to us, and all Wen could think to do was abandon it where it sat, take the Number 11 bus (his two legs) and hitch-hike into the center of town and purloin our work unit taxi. Thus he was gone more than an hour, and you can imagine our worry and surprise also when Chen Tai-pan and his mule arrived back at the work site before the bus did! Chen recounted his dismay at first seeing the bus go sparking and screeching past him, and then finding it at the storage area, wheel rim battered to such a pulp that the idea of simply changing the tire was beyond the realm of possibility.

Naturally we had no idea what had happened to Wen, or where he had disappeared to. I began to grow quite paranoid: he was going to run off with my grand and let the rest of us get caught stealing a shipment of melons bound for Shanghai! I had just about convinced myself of this when Wen finally came screeching up in his taxi, leapt out and began to attack one of the piles of melons we had waiting for him.

"If we do this on a regular basis," Chen said to me as I dropped a melon into his hands, "we'd better get a truck of our own."

"Oh sure," I said. "What's another twenty grand?"

"A used one," he said. "Maybe a Russian one."

"Don't tell me," I said. "We'll buy it from the Pakistanis."

Riding a Tiger

"No," Chen said seriously. "From the Russians."

"All we need is a couple of Japanese motorcycles," I said.

"Right!" Chen said. "How did you know?"

"I'll leave that project to you and Wen," I said. "You find us a good deal and I'll think about it. But I'm not made of dollars, you know."

Tai Hai-yan was doing a damned good job of pitching melons, by the way, and by now she was down to her waist and had first to raise the melons to her chest and shoot them to me like a basketball. Mr. Whiz was already out of sight, but the melons kept floating out of the darkness into Kirby's hands.

"Hey, Kirby!" I yelled.

"Hey, Fisher," he shouted in return.

"Change places with your partner."

"I've been tryin' to, but the sucker hasn't taken a break even yet."

"Don't let him kill himself."

"He don't seem to mind it a bit," Kirby said, grinning away.

In a little while, it was all Hai-yan could do to lift the melons to the rim of the gondola, let alone lob them to me. One, then another failed to make the distance, splattered at the base of the wall.

"O.K.!" I held up my hands. "I'm coming over. You rest, then catch for a while. Hey?"

"I'm tire too much," Hai-yan said.

"I understand. Take it easy."

I climbed down from the wall and into the gondola, twisting an ankle on a melon that rolled, collapsing on top of Hai-yan, who went down under me with a little cry of alarm.

"Are you all right?" I asked her.

Her face was close to mine and — can you imagine it, comrades? — she was laughing! She also kissed my neck.

"I'm die," she said.

"You feel plenty alive to me."

"Please get off," she said. "Melon too hard."

"Of course." I rolled over, tried to find footing and raise myself, went down again. "Shit!"

"Not nice word," Hai-yan said.

"Oh yeah? How do you know?"

"That's what you say every time bus door shuts in your face."

"It's quite a versatile word," I admitted. "My God! It's getting light out. We'd better get humming."

By now Kirby and Mr. Whiz had changed places, and Kirby had apparently determined to see how much Whiz could handle, because he began hurling melons with a vengeance. Tai Hai-yan hauled herself out of the car and scrabbled over the wall, too, after several attempts. In a moment, Ms. Cao stood silhouetted against the lightening sky, so I presumed she had decided to fill in for Hai-yan. As rhythmically as I could, I began to hurl melons. Deep as I was in the gondola now, I couldn't really see how accurate my throws to Ms. Cao were, but at that point I really didn't care. I just heaved and heaved again, and then heaved some more.

Suddenly, the car gave a terrible jerk, and I was nearly knocked over. The blow threw Kirby off balance, too, and he lofted a melon straight into the air that then thudded close to his head.

"God damn," he said, picking himself up, and tossing melons over the side as fast as he could, not making any attempt to reach Mr. Whiz, just trying to get as many melons overboard as possible.

I followed his lead, and had humped a dozen or so when the train banged, lurched, banged again, and we heard a distant short burst of whistle.

"O.K., Kirby," I said. "That does it. Let's get our asses out of here."

"Be right with you," he said, tossing still.

Myself, I went over the side, was given a boost by another tremor that leapt from car to car, crackled like thunder down the line. Ms. Cao was shouting, waving me out of the yard. I gathered melons from the ground and handed them up to her. Now the train began to roll slowly. Kirby, invisible to me, was still popping melons over the side at a steady pace, and they thudded in the cinders. I trotted alongside the car, salvaging melons as I went, called to Kirby.

"Come out of there, you idiot!"

Kirby continued pumping a stream of melons out of the car.

"Come on, Kirby! Out of there!"

The wheels began to grind and squeal now, and the whistle shrilled again, longer, louder.

"Kir-by!"

Ms. Cao and Mr. Whiz and everybody else by this time had begun to chatter hysterically in Chinese, and I really couldn't believe what I was seeing, hoping it was a very bad dream. The cars were humming along nicely now, melons created a steady trail along the tracks, like drops from a leaky faucet, and Kirby still invisible and still whaling away! I threw my hands down in disgust and misery. That goddamn fool was going to Shanghai!

As the cars clanged by, I rounded up the melons close to the wall, and then hauled myself over.

"Your friend!" Ms. Cao asked. "What is he doing?"

"He's not my friend," I said. "He's nuts. He'll be heaving melons from here to the Huang Po!"

Now we had plenty of melons on the street, and at a taxi-load and a cart-load at a time, the pile was not diminishing too goddamn fast, believe me. Not only that, we were also saddled with the problem of getting a bus repaired and back into service by 8 AM. For that reason, I had Wen take Mr. Whiz with him on the next trip out to see what the two of them might be able to do to get the machine back in service and save Chen Tai-pan's neck, maybe even keep us all from getting arrested for bus theft. I was tired, I was nearly in despair, and I sat down — plunk! — on top of a pile of melons and wished myself dead. What a fiasco!

The other men were gone, of course, delivering melons, driving a mule, fixing a bus, one fool riding off to God knows where. There was nothing to do but wait. Another hour and the sun would be up, and we'd have to leave whatever there was to be left right where it was. Already the traffic was picking up and pedestrians and cyclists were eyeing us and our melon pile with disgruntled curiosity. We may even have sold a few at colossal discount because cracked by rough handling.

Then Tai Hai-yan presented me with a chunk of broken melon and sat down next to me. And Ms. Cao sat beside me, too, on the other side, and without saying anything, we continued to break apart this melon, and share it, slaking our thirst in its wonderful sweetness, spitting the seeds shamelessly onto the sidewalk.

Comrades!

I was happy.

8

WE HAVE A QUESTION or two about yesterday's testimony.
 I'm not surprised. I'm not nearly finished with this particular episode.
 Did "Mr. Whiz" fix the bus?
 Oh yes. He finished that chore about nine o'clock.
 What is a "Velcro fastener"?
 It's a fastener made from bristles, plastic bristles. The bristles lock together. You know what a burr is? It's like burrs sticking together.
 Who was Cassandra?
 Right. That comes from Greek legend. Cassandra was a prophetess. She speaks the truth, but no one believes her.
 What happened to Mr. Kirby?
 I don't know. A couple of days later he was back at Café Nº 1, same as ever. He never even mentioned it. He just looked at me, kind of roosterish, smiled and nodded. I'll bet he unloaded that gondola, though.
 Were you able to remove all the melons from the street?
 As a matter of fact, we almost did. We got real selective, though, and left the badly broken ones behind. It wasn't a neat job.
 What happened afterwards?
 Afterwards? After all that work? Why are you asking this? What could possibly have happened?
 Answer the question, please.
 Well, hell. Believe it or not, Tai Hai-yan and Mr. Whiz went to work at the petroleum refinery. Mr. Wen also went to work, though I suspect he found a shady place to park the taxi and took a good nap. I think Chen told me he took a nap and then went to work after lunch.
 That leaves you and Ms. Cao.
 Well. Yeah.
 Yes?
 You could level with me, you know. You could tell me what you already know.
 All we want is the truth.
 So what did Ms. Cao say about this particular morning after a night of loading melons? You have her self-criticism, I presume.
 Our records indicate she went to your hotel rooms.

Well, that is correct, comrades. Quite correct. As you can imagine, we were completely grimy, and after we taxied Tai Hai-yan to her dormitory, Ms. Cao expressed fear that her husband would be awake by now and she would have a hell of a time explaining her battered looks. So I suggested she come to the hotel and take a quick shower and taxi from there back home, or to work, whatever she wanted to do.

So Ms. Cao came to my hotel room with a paper bag in which she had a dress and shoes to change into once she got out of her slacks and sweater and sneakers. Always practical! She was embarrassed to come through the lobby and pass the attendants there, especially since we both looked like coal miners, and it made me a little nervous, too, wondering what the gossip along the corridor would be a few minutes after the door to my room was closed and the "Do Not Disturb" sign was swinging from the knob.

Because she was my "guest," Ms. Cao absolutely would not shower before I did. She refused adamantly, and so I made up a little tea and cut her a few slices of breakfast bread I had stashed in a drawer, which she practically inhaled. I took my shower and dressed in pajamas and robe — intending, you see, to kiss off the morning at work, figuring I had put in plenty of extra hours and had some time coming anyway. Really, I was almost too tired to stand up and towel myself off.

Now I know that for all her sophistication and her two years in America, Ms. Cao was really not familiar with our Western appliances. I made it a point to remind her how the shower and toilet worked, and then I shut the door, and she locked it, and I sat in a chair and nodded off.

I woke when Ms. Cao came out of the bathroom. Her hair was down, and wet, and she was combing it out with some difficulty. Wet, her hair shone, and it seemed to weigh about forty pounds, and there was so much of it, so much that she kept hidden from the world. She had removed her glasses and her face looked sleepy and vulnerable, no longer composed and official. She had also slipped on her dress for modesty's sake, but because she had not dried herself well, the dress clung to her skin with what I thought, comrades, was a very appealing effect. She was neither as tall nor as robust as Tai Hai-yan, but she had surprisingly full hips after all, and lovely shoulders, and it was all I could do to keep from putting my arms (which I could hardly lift anyway) around her, out of pure affection.

She sat in a chair opposite me, leaned forward to pull at her hair, drops spotting the floor, knees tight together. Then I realized that she had been watching me through a veil of hair, and I looked away, embarrassed.

"Fisher!" she said.

"Yes?"

"I think you like me."

"There's no question about that."

"Maybe," she said, combing still, "you would like to have a Chinese wife, a number two wife."

"Yes."

She parted her hair with her hands, swept it over her shoulders, looked directly at me.

"Would I do?"

"Please. Yes."

She held out her hands. My old heart thundered. I proved to be slightly less exhausted than I thought I was.

9

WE WANT TO KNOW the exact nature of your relationship with Ms. Cao. We also want to know more about Chen Tai-pan, what you meant when you told us to notice closely that he suggested you buy your own truck.

That's right! I did say that, didn't I?

Well, as I think you are now aware, comrades, unloading a gondola of watermelons in three hours, then transporting it all to our storage sites, was more than our crew could handle. We left a lot of melons on the train (or along the tracks, thanks to Kirby), but even so the margin of profit was great enough for me to recoup my losses and dispense token shares in our tiny profits. I think Ms. Cao figured we had probably made about six cents an hour on that particular venture. We recognized that every broken melon and every melon we did not unload from the gondola represented money that might have been in our hands. And it was a sufficient amount of potential money to rekindle our enthusiasm. I think it was a bit like having the big fish slip off the hook just as you are about to land him in the net. We almost blew it, but we had also learned a lot.

We counseled over the matter. We needed temporary, direct help to unload the gondola; we needed a good, reliable truck; we needed a place to keep the truck. Chen Tai-pan suggested that when we were not using the truck ourselves, we could rent it, and by that means help pay for it. It was this idea that persuaded me to dig even deeper into my jeans. All right, then, Chen and Wen would find us a truck, Ms. Cao and Tai Hai-yan would recruit for us some temporary unloading help. Mr. Whiz, when necessary, would repair our truck and make sure it was in prime condition when we needed it. Everyone was discreetly to seek truck rental customers.

Now, comrades, as you know, and as I had been aware since the start of my bicycle business, China has not yet developed a good economic mechanism for dealing with the sale of used goods. So this also has become a fairly shadowy realm. Besides that, there is a limited supply of vehicles, and limited space to keep them in, and very strict licensing regulations, so that even if you are lucky enough to find a used truck and can buy it, it comes equipped with a host of problems. Chen Tai-pan was very philosophical about this, and I treasure the memory of his remarking, "a problem that cannot be solved is not a problem. It is a condition."

And conditions, obviously, are something you must simply live with, or live around.

Now the difficult conditions of buying a good used truck led Chen and Wen back to the money-changers and the Silk Road network that led also to Russian trucks. Not incidentally, I had entrusted these two men with quite a bit of US cash, I mean enough to rouse the interests of any genuine thugs who might get wind of a big cash deal in the making. I'm afraid that the amount of cash involved also proved too tempting for Wen himself, who apparently thought he could skim a little for some quick investments in rape (the vegetable) and tomatoes and make up the difference out of the profits in jig time. If Wen has offered up a self-criticism, you probably know more about this than I do. The point is this, comrades: the search for a truck led Chen and Wen into contact with some fairly grisly criminal types, some of whom were not the least bit happy — or may have been looking for an excuse not to be happy — when Wen came up short on cash and promised the rest later. The truck dealers were not a credit operation, as they made clear. Severe deadlines were set. I'm guessing here, comrades, because Wen never told me the whole truth and didn't have a chance to tell me the whole story. Neither did Chen Tai-pan.

God damn it!

The Murphy/Zhang Law must have struck Wen, too. Perfect weather. Rape and tomatoes flourished. The prices fell. Here was a capitalist wrinkle no one had told Wen about, the problem of what we call "selling short", associated with commodities trading. Wen took a beating, the first financial, the second literal.

Comrades! Tell me if I'm wrong, I beg you, but did Wen Da-xing or did he not, try to save his own neck with the truck dealers by assigning the blame for the short payment to Chen Tai-pan?

Or did the gangsters simply get Mr. Wen and Mr. Chen confused?

Or was some other force at work?

Well, then, we got our truck, all of us except Wen innocent of the troubles it was loaded with, and would dump upon us. We were not so innocent of the need for parking space, however, and some semblance of legal papers to operate our new treasure. The quest for these essentials opened new doors into subterranean Beijing.

But perhaps my first duty here, for the record, is to report on the curious process of finally getting our truck, an adventure I will never forget. As I mentioned, I had risked a stupendous amount by anyone's standards and while I trusted Chen and Wen (the latter overmuch, I fear),

I really had no control over or even any knowledge of where my money was going and whether we'd ever really see a truck at all. Wen insisted that I had nothing to worry about, that it was all being handled by members of his family, but even so, his reports on the progress of the deal were sketchy and not exactly calming.

Then one night Wen came to my hotel room. Tai Hai-yan happened to be there, absorbed in an English grammar book and eating an orange, and Wen, for reasons of his own, asked me to step outside a moment and sit in the taxi. There he told me the deposit on the truck had been accepted and that the truck itself would be delivered to a little village about fifty kilometers outside of Da Tong. Why Da Tong, a coal-mining city also known for the Yun Gang Caves filled with enormous sandstone Buddhas carved right into the mountainsides, I could not begin to guess. Out there in the desert sticks we would have to take care of a few other details, Wen said.

"Must pay more," he said.

"Sure. You got the money, so do it."

"I can't go," he said.

"Shit."

He handed me a clipboard and pointed to a few items, as if I could actually read them anyway. "When truck goes to Zuotian, I must drive Guangzhou. Orders." He tapped the papers with his fingers. "Also too long for taxi. Takes too long time."

"Why in God's name are they delivering to Zuotian?"

"Maybe half way," Wen said. "Also safe."

"Damn!"

"You take train," Wen said. "Like tourist to see the cave. Come Da Tong, my cousin find you, drive you Zuotian." The plan he sketched out struck me as bizarre as hell, and it was going to take me a long weekend to pull it off — something I didn't think the work unit would especially appreciate.

"I don't know if my Chinese is good enough to handle this," I said.

"Cousin speak little English," Wen said.

"Everybody speaks a little, 'hello' 'good-bye', like that."

"No sweat," Wen said. "My cousin take you Zuotian, paint you truck license."

I took it Wen meant that his cousin would somehow stencil license plate numbers on the truck's tailgate, the most common method of identification. The regional code for Beijing is 01- followed by five numbers: prerogative of the capital city. Tell me, comrades, if these details are not correct?

"And then," I said, "what am I supposed to do? drive the truck back?"

"Sure."

"What's going to happen when the road police see a *weiguoren* wheeling a Beijing truck along the highways and byways of China?"

"Maybe you wear turban."

"Right. I look about as Moslem as I do Chinese."

"No other way," Wen said with a deep shrug, slumping down in the seat. "No?"

"If I can think of any other way — and I mean any — we'll do it," I said. "Believe me, I didn't come to China to risk my neck just to sell a few thousand watermelons."

"No?" Wen smiled wickedly.

He added something in Chinese then, which I caught as *Ji hu rongyi, xia hu nan.* I let it pass, but said "No!" as emphatically as I could to his insolent question. We sat in silence a while and then I asked Wen when he could return the money I'd need for the second payment on the truck.

"My cousin has," he said. "In Da Tong. You get money there."

I nodded, a little worried, you see, not only about the money but the whole deal. I mean, it was going to tax the limits of my Chinese just to read the road signs! I knew enough of the language to ask directions, but that didn't necessarily mean that I could understand the answers I got, especially if given in a dialect. And where the hell was I going to buy gas when I needed it? No question about it, I was going to have to take someone Chinese along with me.

When I returned to the hotel room, Tai Hai-yan was sitting on the end of the bed watching a Donald Duck/Mickey Mouse show on television. Mickey and Donald, I noticed, had learned fluent Mandarin. I flopped on the bed behind Hai-yan and told her what had transpired in the taxi. Hai-yan remained absorbed in the tube.

I asked her "What the hell does *'Jihu rongyi, xiahu nan'* mean?"

She hesitated just a moment, then pronounced the phrase with the correct tones. "I think you mean 'Riding tiger easy, but getting off — hard.' Common saying. How you learn this?"

"Wen said it."

"Yea," Hai-yan replied.

"What do you think?" I asked her. "Am I nuts to make this trip?"

"Maybe I go with you," she said absently.

"Really? Could you? It might be dangerous."

"I am strong," she said.
"Could you really get a couple of extra days off?"
"Maybe."
"Find out, will you? We have to leave this weekend."
She fell back slowly, nestled her head on my chest. I began to stroke her hair, ran the tip of a finger over the outline of her lips. She sucked my finger in, then kissed my hand and placed it on her breast.
She laughed. "Mickey Donald so funny."
"Are they?"
"You don't like."
"I like you."
"I know," she said, smiling. "So why are you sad?"
"Do I sound sad?"
"Yes."
"Maybe because I'm so old and you're so young."
"Not too old," Hai-yan said, twisting to face, and kiss me.
How can it be, comrades, that with the quacking, clatter, Dixieland music and general blather of the cartoon show in our ears, we can yet be transported, awash in love and desire? It was not the sound track I would have chosen, but it seemed to suit Hai-yan just fine. We did everything we could, comrades, short of that consummate act, and when I left her at the bus stop I felt as alone as if I'd been flung out among the stars. After the heat, the glow of our passionate exercise, my room was just too cold to bear. I climbed on my bicycle and rode round and round the hotel grounds. Anyone who dared cross my path was treated to a vigorous ringing of my little bell and an American curse. I exhausted myself sufficiently this way that I could simply fling myself into bed and sleep without any more thinking, just as I had planned.
Without Tai Hai-yan, comrades, I would never had made it to and from Da Tong alive. Why is it so difficult to accomplish what should be simple things, like buying a train ticket, or reserving a hotel room? It's not the travel that exhausts one in China, but the hassle, the argument, the rudeness, the uncertainty of every transaction.
We'd like to get a soft sleeper to Da Tong.
Mei you. (No got.)
O.K., hard sleeper then.
Mei you.
Soft seats to Da Tong?
Mei you.
Hard seats, then.

Mei you.

We've just exhausted all the possibilities of seating. You don't mean to say there is no train at all to Da Tong?

Mei you.

I know damn well there is a regular train to Da Tong, comrades, and you know it, too. Furthermore, it even runs on time, as a rule, and to be told there is no such train or there are no seats of any kind available is infuriating beyond belief. We storm out of the Beijing train station, the special section reserved for foreign travelers, stew for an hour, and then return, armed with righteous anger.

We'd like a soft sleeper to Da Tong.

Yes sir.

This weekend. Friday night.

Of course, sir.

I'm going to be traveling with my secretary. I'd like to reserve two beds.

As you wish, sir.

I'm not going to pay FEC or US currency. I have a white card and I'm paying *renminbi*.

Excellent, sir.

Is this the same station? Am I actually talking to the same clerk? Is this the same planet? What has happened in the last sixty minutes to change all the *mei you*s to *yes sir*s? Everyone pretends that the clerk was not thoroughly rude and obstructionist and that the foreign expert was not in a towering rage so close to murder that he had to walk out in order not to commit mayhem. Now everything is hunky-dory. America and China are the closest of friends. We actually have tickets in our hands and they say on them what we want them to say: soft sleeper to Da Tong, Friday. Life is grand!

Thank you, comrade.

Think nothing of it.

Will you marry me?

Of course, sir. Right away, sir.

My boots. They need to be licked.

Don't worry, sir. We'll see to it.

And my shorts? I'd like someone to bite them.

Right away, sir.

Any chance of a private compartment? You see, my secretary and I, well, we'll need to take care of some business before reaching Da Tong,

and it would be convenient if we could be alone and enhance China's four modernizations.
   No problem!
   A little champagne on ice?
   Assuredly.
   Comrades! Forgive this vengeful little fantasy, but it is the inevitable reaction to insult, frustration, and just never knowing whether a decision is capricious or grounded in necessity. Of course the train to Da Tong might have been filled to capacity and, in consequence, an hour later more cars were added to accommodate the demand. A word to that effect would have spared considerable rage, would it not? The contemporary history of China being what it has been, we do not expect the Chinese to greet *weiguoren,* your former exploiters, with leis and song. And perhaps, after all, we only get what the rest of China gets from a railway clerk or salesperson in the neighborhood store. If so, what a wearying country! What a waste of energy! All we ask is a little information and a little courtesy.
   Hai-yan was tremendously excited about the trip, excited and anxious. She had never been to Da Tong before and had heard from Mr. Whiz that it was an arid, forbidding place, a brawling, coal-mining town. She packed sensibly — just a small bag — and dressed in the cheerful colors she liked so much. We negotiated the tumult in the station, stepping over the legs and torsos of people who were napping on their bundles, and found our car. The conductors were extremely courteous, even though they checked and rechecked Hai-yan's ticket, since it was unusual to mix foreigners and Chinese.
   We had hoped to have the car to ourselves, but knew this was foolish. We sat on one of the lower bunks discreetly touching hands, but were soon joined by an Australian couple my age, a very businesslike pair. They were also used to traveling in China and were not bothered by the presence of strangers in their sleeping quarters. Fortunately, they were also not voluble people and after the usual exchange of pleasantries — he was in refrigeration, she, a piano teacher — we climbed into our racks, Hai-yan and I taking the upper berths.
   For some reason you Chinese feel it necessary to bombard your rail passengers continuously with news, slogans, entertainment and patriotic songs. Do you not trust us to have a thought of our own? This high-volume intrusion on one's sanity continued until eleven o'clock and then, mercifully, ceased. I lay on my side in the bunk and watched Hai-yan

settle into sleep. A beautiful kid, truly! There was only a meter between us, and yet it seemed a distance of centuries.

You know what it's like to sleep on a train, comrades. I woke when the train stopped, and sometimes the train seemed to have stopped for good, as if we had mistakenly been shunted off to some siding. I also kept dreaming that someone intruded into the compartment, but when I awoke all was well and quiet, the train trembling and clacking. Very early dawn, I rolled over and saw that Hai-yan was awake and watching me, covers pulled to her chin. We blew each other kisses, and, abstract as they were, they excited me. How I wished we were alone!

The countryside around Da Tong was sparse with trees, gravely, earth the color of camel's hair. A semi-circle of worn hills half-surrounded the city, but otherwise it was a flat place. As we neared the city, we saw mounds of coal as tall as the factory buildings they were heaped next to, and a bustle of blue trucks along the highways. We passed gondola after gondola heaped with coal and the closer we came to the city the more the patina of coal dust was evident, until the buildings seemed made of black brick and the camel-colored earth seemed burned to ash.

We stepped out of the train into sunshine so bright it almost blinded me. We had been unloaded on a concrete island and were swept along by the crowd into a tunnel that took us beneath the tracks and then up into an austere lobby. Here we detached ourselves from the crowd as best we could and waited, hungry and anxious, for Wen's cousin.

Half an hour passed and the lobby was almost empty of traffic. A few customers passed by the ticket windows and the only other people in view were a policeman and a pair of taxi drivers. The taxi drivers both pestered us and seemed miffed when we turned them down. We milled a little, especially since I was growing nervous about the scrutiny of the policeman, and ended up outside the front entrance, morning sun already at a withering intensity. I took the hat Ms. Cao had given me out of my travel bag and slapped it on.

Now a motorcycle came crackling into the parking area, driven by a man as short and stout as myself wearing a white robe and a turban of the style that seems to be made of a ring of thick, braided rope and skull cap. The motorcycle banged out puffs of blue and black exhaust and its brakes screeched demonically when the rider pulled up before us.

"Fish-ah!" he called.

"Yes!"

He pointed to the seat behind him, actually just an extension of the seat he was sitting on, and barely large enough for a child. "Come ride."

"Wait a minute," I said, and with Hai-yan, I approached the man and explained that I had a companion.

The man was openly indignant and flabbergasted. His English was as bad as my Chinese and so we all found it easier to let Hai-yan translate. He was a very nervous fellow, tugged at the black hair that coursed over his ears and constantly grimaced. His cousin Wen had said nothing about a girl and thus our would-be chauffeur seemed determined to believe she didn't exist. His inflexibility began to grate.

"We'll take a taxi," I said. "We'll meet you."

The man explained that he had intended to motorcycle me to Zuotian. He didn't even know anyone with a private car.

"What's wrong with hiring one of the taxi guys for a day?" I asked.

"He says," Hai-yan translated, "he doesn't want them to know his business or where he's taking you."

"What about another motorcycle? I could handle that."

"Who would bring it back, he wants to know."

"We'll deliver it in the truck."

"He says no way. No Russian truck can be seen in Da Tong."

"Tell him it's obvious I need your help. I'm not going anywhere without you."

The man seemed especially disturbed by this report.

"He says," Hai-yan related, "women and business no good mix. Also he says truck is in a mosque. I cannot enter."

"Well fuck a duck."

"I don't understand this meaning."

"Thank heaven. But God damn it, wouldn't you think at least the *illegal* activity in China would be free of bureaucratic snafu? I wonder what he'd say if I just demanded my money back."

"Should I question?"

"Yeah. Run that by him."

Hai-yan did as I asked. The man bristled, then barked, "You wait!" and I'll be damned if he didn't engage the clutch and go popping and banging off into the city.

"Now what the hell?" I wondered aloud.

"I don't know," Hai-yan said with an exasperated shrug.

"At least let's get something to eat. If he comes back real soon, *he* can wait."

We crossed a parking lot and entered a street of small, one-story, open-to-the-air shops, looking for a restaurant. Instead, we found a little free market, a line of tables heaped with clothes, bottles, and food under thin, striped canopies that did little to block the force of the sun. We bought some tea-boiled eggs (duck eggs, I assumed) and some steamed buns — two items I hoped would be cooked sufficiently well to be safe. I know what Krazy Kirby would have said, and even Hai-yan was a little skeptical.

"Street food sometimes not safe."

"I don't see any alternatives close by."

Hai-yan questioned the women selling the food and chose to trust them. The women were an animated bunch, mostly elderly, heads wrapped in kerchiefs, and very curious about me. One ran off into a nearby *hutong* and returned with a camera to take my picture. Through Hai-yan I answered questions about myself, and America. They tried to sell me everything. I was a little flattered, of course, but mostly I felt plagued. I just wanted to get my truck and get the hell out of there. Odds were, I was beginning to think, Hai-yan and I were just going to be taking the next train back. And what the hell was all this business about anyway? Moving a few watermelons around! Some people, somehow, manage to do great things, win great awards and serve humanity well, earn the respect of all humankind. But me, comrades, and a lot of people like me, I think, I just keep painting myself into weird little corners, and wondering how I got there.

The eggs and the steamed bread lay in my belly like a wet towel. Ugh! I noticed Hai-yan fed half her bun to a persistent white duck that had taken a liking to her, and her course seemed the only sensible one. I waited to see if the duck would die, like a miner's canary — just joking, comrades! — and tried to smile for the camera of the little old lady trinket seller.

We made our way back to the train station after an hour of desultory walking along the streets of Da Tong. Hai-yan talked about the Yun Gang caves, and I thought it would be interesting to see them — Buddhas as tall as buildings? — carved by a mad monk? — isn't that the sort of thing I really came to China to see? Now it aggravated me even more that I had allowed myself, trapped myself, more like it, into playing the entrepreneur and was so snarled in this watermelon business that I was not even free to do a little sight-seeing!

We sat on the curb before the train terminal like a couple of beggars and waited. Oddly, the thought of all my money disappearing down the Silk Road did not infuriate me. What I felt was more like *stupid* and oppressed, not that I didn't intend to give Wen a good piece of my mind when I returned. About noon, just after Hai-yan and I had made another foray out for food — this time to a grocery store for oranges and cookies — Hai-yan and I guessed it would be pretty futile to try to track down Wen's cousin (we didn't even know his name), and made the decision to buy our return tickets to Beijing.

I had just dusted off my trouser bottom when one of your celebrated two-wheel tractors — the "double-banger" with the huge flywheel constantly spinning, surely the drive for many a country machine, from pulley systems to grain grinders — came roaring into the parking lot. Behind this tractor was a flat, wooden cart on two oversized wheels and the little old driver (so lively and quick) was none other than Wen's nervous cousin. He took another complete swing around the parking lot before he figured out how to disengage the engine and operate the brake, then slammed to a halt and waved us aboard. The taxi drivers lounging by the entrance were volubly outraged, and Wen's cousin was made all the more anxious and impatient by their outcries.

We leapt aboard, Hai-yan with her cookies and travel bag, me with my shoulder satchel. From the smell of our transport I would say that its most recent cargo had been crates of live chickens, and we had not even a sack of grain or bale of straw between us and the rough lumber the trailer was constructed of.

Kapakita pak pak pak, the engine sang, and we were suddenly sailing down the dusty Da Tong streets, narrowly missing cyclists, battling for road space with those tremendous, coal-laden blue trucks. Our cart registered every imperfection in the road surface with a crash. It is fair to say, comrades, that my poor old ass was getting a righteous pounding.

Wen's cousin wheeled along in manic silence, sensibly making no attempt to compete with the unfettered *pakity pakity* of the tractor engine. I figured Wen himself was probably cruising the highway in air-conditioned comfort enjoying the beauties of Guangzhou, amiably conversing with our work unit colleagues and looking forward to a belly-filling lunch and a nice nap. *If* he had told the truth. I determined to check this out when I returned, no doubt blinded by dust, deafened by engine roar, and lame from the battering. "Oh? And how was your trip to Guangzhou?"

Da Tong center, small as it is, we escaped in a short time. Just outside the city we were cruising along a road that intersected a wide expanse of railroad tracks, and along these tracks a huge black and red steam engine burying itself in billows of white smoke like a true dragon was thundering ahead. Remembering the difficulty Wen's cousin had in stopping his tractor at the train station, I began to grow a little faint as it became more apparent with the acceleration of the *pakity paks* that our be-turbaned driver was actually racing the enormous Marching Forward engine to the crossing!

"You yokel!" I raged, but Wen's cousin seemed to take this for encouragement and turned the throttle all the way up.

I thought of my wife, my dear wife, my daughter, my mother, all of whom would be asking "Why?" and receiving the answer, "Watermelons."

Hai-yan calmly handed me a cookie.

We slammed across the intersection, the rails tossing the cart like a ship in a storm, under the nose of the Marching Forward, our "victory" sung by a bone-quivering shriek from the train's whistle. Wen's cousin was grinning from ear to ear, but I was filled with the oddest mixture of outrage and nausea. The horrible thought crossed my mind that on top of everything else I was going to be motion-sick. The cookie Hai-yan had given me was now nothing but a mass of sweaty crumbs in the palm of my hand.

Away from the city and the mines, the ride became smoother. We entered even more truly desert country, a formidable dry, rocky terrain as unbroken as the sea. (Should I rewrite that last line, comrades? Is it self-consciously "literary"?) I was glad for my hat, for the sun was by now merciless, and drops of sweat stood out on Hai-yan's brow. We were also, all of us, being caked with dust. I prayed we should not run out of gas. Not here, dear Lord!

I said little about Da Tong, comrades, because I presume that many of you are familiar with it, but I might say a little more about Zuotian because it is off the beaten track and unlikely that you have visited there. Indeed it is hard to imagine why anyone even lives in such a place, or how those that do, survive. My guess is that about six hundred people inhabit the village and that their economy is based about ten per cent on passers-by who stumble into this god-forsaken byway and ninety per cent on neighborhood barter. Comrades! I do not exaggerate when I say that to these spoiled Western eyes, the people and the vegetables for sale in the free market there seemed equally wizened. The thought of being cast adrift in a city like this took my breath away.

I was choked with dust when we clattered in and happy to see a large tea shop on one street corner with tables and chairs neatly arranged on the inevitable brick patio. The village seemed to exist primarily along the main street, which boasted raised wooden sidewalks (why? It could conceivably never be muddy there) and in the very center a once-Buddhist temple of four stories, arched windows and sloping tile roof. The spire of this ancient building now carried a rusting red star. One-story shops hugged the boardwalk, some sharing interior walls but many also isolated, or existing at the entrance to *hutong*s hidden by antique "spirit gates" — the kind which are designed to prevent demons, which travel in straight lines, from entering the neighborhood.

We blasted into an alley between a shop selling bronze goods (Mongolian hot pots gleamed in the window), and another selling watches and false teeth, pictures of each painted on each side of the open entranceway. The alley itself was narrow with a nasty little ditch running down the middle of it. A little black pig slithered out of our way and through a gate. Wen's cousin shut off the tractor engine and the comparative silence that enveloped us was delicious. Also delicious was the shade of the building, and my first communication with our driver since the tedious, battering ride began was to ask for tea.

"Yes, yes," he said, with a wave of impatience. "Inside now."

Hai-yan and I dismounted eagerly, but also gingerly, sore all over. Wen's cousin hustled us out of sight as quickly as he could, for reasons that were to become clear only a short while later. Now we entered a dark, bare room with muslin sheets draped over open windows. Two men in fezzes sat at a round table exchanging a long, thin pipe with a small bowl. Commands were shouted to an adjoining room and a female voice responded.

"They make some tea now," Hai-yan said.

The men at the table, both slender with walnut dark skin that reminded me of American Indians and secretive faces did not rise but gave curt bows in greeting. In a moment, two chairs appeared and Hai-yan and I sat, more out of politeness than out of desire. The smoke from the pipe drifted in lazy layers in the diffuse light of the windows. The men said nothing, inspected us askance as they continued to smoke. Presently a large woman came bustling into the room, placed a teapot and cups on the table and immediately struck up an enthusiastic conversation with Hai-yan. Her curiosity about the two of us was just too overwhelming to be contained and as she spoke her eyes widened and glittered, and she also laughed in an easy, utterly familiar way that helped a little to put me at ease. She nattered steadily for a while, responded to Hai-yan's answers with an "Oh! Oh!" that was soft as a peach, a voice both sympathetic and curious, until the men dismissed her.

The tea was piping, and I drank mine too quickly, apologized via Hai-yan by saying the desert ride had made me thirsty.

The men grunted their understanding, poured more tea. Wen's cousin did most of the talking, meanwhile, and I could tell from his hand gestures and the noises he made that he was boasting about his race with the train. Neither of the men responded to these heroics and when Wen's cousin finished bragging the room was silent again. We continued to drink tea in this silence for an agonizingly long time.

Finally I asked when I could see the truck.

They muttered answers and Hai-yan told me, "It is being made ready now. Make license."

Wen's cousin left, and this troubled me because I had assumed — or hoped at least — that he would be supplying much, if not all of the money we would be turning over for the truck. For all I knew we were in the midst of a colossal scam, an Oriental version of the old Murphy game with the truck substituting for the always non-existent "whore". The only assurance I had to the contrary was that, in the event of a sting, I could always lay hands on the set-up man, Wen himself, who daily chauffeured me around Beijing. But then, without a truck, how the hell would we ever get out of Zuotian?

Growing more nervous minute by silent minute, I asked Hai-yan if I should be doing something, saying something.

"Just wait," she said. "These men are traditional Chinese. No hurry to work."

"But I would like to get out of here before dark."

"I will run by them with this," Hai-yan said and apparently passed my concerns on. "Just wait for Wen's cousin, they say. No hurry."

Come to think of it, I hadn't heard the tractor start up again, and that gave me one reason to imagine that Wen's cousin wasn't hell bent for Xinjiang with my cash. And in a moment he in fact returned with a dramatic slap of the muslin curtain. After a little banter which had them all smiling, Wen's cousin produced a round, metal tin and placed it in the hands of the oldest man at the table. In turn, this man pried off the lid and slowly counted the money inside — US dollars and FEC, from what I could see. A rather disgruntled look came over his face, and he called to the woman beyond the curtain. She delivered an abacus, disappeared, and the old man painstakingly counted the money again. Then he pushed the tin into the center of the table and shot an angry inquiry at Wen's cousin.

"He says not enough," Hai-yan told me.

"Why not enough?" I groaned. "I mean, is there not enough money in the tin, or does he just want a bigger portion of the total now?"

Wen's cousin's replies to the two men behind the table were apparently not satisfactory, and in a moment all three were heatedly arguing, banging the table, spitting. Wen's cousin stood up and reclaimed the tin, but after some more high volume shouting returned it to the table.

Finally Wen's cousin turned to Hai-yan and ticking off several items on his fingers, spoke rapidly to her. Then he stood and motioned for us to leave.

"What's going on?" I asked her.

"They need to discuss why not enough money," Hai-yan said. "Family matter, so we must wait outside a little."

"I don't like this," I said. "I feel a sting coming on. A big one. I'll bet you anything in about five minutes Wen's cousin will come out and ask me for more money."

We found ourselves on the boardwalk not far, and across the street from the busy tea shop.

"You don't trust those men?" Hai-yan asked.

A man driving a mule past on the street almost fell off his cart when he saw us. His jaw dropped and his eyes remained fixed on me until his head had swiveled nearly one hundred eighty degrees.

"You watch. Five minutes, and they'll ask for more money. If I give it to them, we'll probably be waiting for them forever."

"Why?"

"I'm beginning to think there's no truck, just tricks."

"No!"

"Well, they're not getting any more money from me. You can tell them that. I gave the right amount to Wen, and if it didn't get through, then he's the one responsible. But no more dough from me."

In another moment, I noticed that the man who had just passed in the cart was walking toward us with three or four others, presumably from the tea shop, since that is where the driver's rig now stood. This chorus of citizens in dusty blue Mao suits and caps lined up before us, hands folded in front or behind them, and simply stared. One of the men cleared his throat and spoke to Hai-yan. She laughed and responded.

"He asked if I speak Chinese!" she laughed.

The old man asked another question, which Hai-yan answered with an obvious "no," but also with laughter.

"He wants to know am I *actress*. I said I am only from Beijing."

The men discussed this. When they were talking, Wen's cousin stepped out, motioned me into the entranceway, and, as I feared, asked me for what amounted to almost another grand. Hai-yan conveyed my message to him. I made it clear there was no argument. I had given Wen the true amount. If the right amount was not here, someone else was responsible. Wen's cousin tried a little belligerence, pressing against me and shaking his finger in my face, but I lifted him off the ground and gave him the most Bogartish voice I could manage: "You're nuts, pal, if you think you can Murphy me!" Nobody understood the words but me, but everyone understood my meaning. Wen's cousin picked my hands off his clothing and slunk inside, leaving me breathing hard with a little adrenaline rush. When Hai-yan and I stepped back onto the boardwalk we were now greeted with about fifty pairs of eyes.

The old man who had spoken before spoke again.

"He wants to know if everyone in Beijing wears such pretty clothes," she said. "They never see a city girl. They want to know who makes my shoes."

The old man asked another question that caused the crowd to titter. Hai-yan answered vigorously, with obvious indignation.

"He wants to know if I wear underthings!" she said, blushing, piqued. "Can you imagine?"

The old man continued to ask questions, prompted by the crowd, which continued to grow. I heard the phrase *yang gui zi* — "foreign ghost".

"Is difficult dialect," Hai-yan said. "I don't understand all his meaning."

In Mandarin I said, "I'm not a foreign ghost. I'm a foreign expert."

This shocked the crowd into a stunned silence, and stunned me, too, for now they appeared genuinely frightened of me. After a moment, the old man queried Hai-yan again.

"I told them you were an American, from Boston. You have wife and daughter. You are computer man."

"No, no. Tell them I am a fisherman."

"Don't lie to them. No!"

"But I am a fisherman," I said.

"Really?"

"Yes."

Hai-yan passed this information on and my impression was that the crowd relaxed a little, that I was seen more as a curiosity and not so much as a monstrosity. But how can I know what they thought? The situation just suddenly seemed less tense to me.

"Oh dear," Hai-yan said. "He asks if all Americans have fat."

"Tell him many do, but not all. Tell him we are well fed but don't always eat the best things."

Before this profound news could be communicated, Wen's cousin was again motioning me inside. Through Hai-yan, this is what I learned: There simply was not the agreed upon amount in the tin, and so Wen must have diverted or borrowed some of the funds. Wen's cousin could in no conceivable way make up the difference, at least not on the spot. The truck was ready to roll, however. Therefore, if I would be willing to take the truck, loaded half with garlic and half with cabbages, to Beijing, sell the produce and turn over *all* the proceeds to Wen (for return to these men), the deal could go down today.

"Well, I'll be damned," I said, genuinely miffed. I knew one thing for sure. When I returned, I was going to wring Wen's neck. Who the hell did he think he was, cutting himself a grand out of my truck deposit? And he could jolly well sell the vegetables himself! "O.K.," I said. "Let's do it. Let's get the truck loaded and get the hell out of here."

We re-entered the dark inner sanctum, shook hands, made toasts all around with tea. Hai-yan and I begged use of the toilet and afterwards left by the back door and remounted out torturing carriage. When we swung out onto the street we could see the crowd was still where it had been, patiently waiting for another glimpse of the Beijing actress and the foreign ghost. But we were *pakity-pak-pak*ing out of their lives, and I was damned glad of it.

Comrades! When the doors of the garage were flung open (had it been moved from the mosque, or was the mosque business some sort of dodge?) and I was confronted with our pale blue, gleaming 1948 (I'm guessing, but that's a reasonable estimate of its vintage) Russian *Danska*, I didn't know whether to laugh or to cry. For all its antiquity and a few minor dents, it still appeared new, and when I tossed open the hood (no easy matter!) and checked out the engine, I found even that was spotless: a straight v-8, no frills. The beast started with a *pop!* shivered, rumbled authoritatively. The gears chinked solidly into place. I was completely satisfied.

And so, comrades, with Wen's cousin leading the way on the tractor, Hai-yan and I rolled out of Zuotian to a dusty little commune in the nearby hills. The houses — sheds? cottages? — here were made of rocks the size of softballs and roofed over with a kind of cane, some thick, hollow-stalked plant I couldn't identify and didn't have time to ask about given the uproarious bustle that followed our arrival. As the truck was loaded with speed and coordination even in that blistering sun that our watermelon crew could have learned something from, Hai-yan scribbled down directions to Beijing. I lounged proprietarily by the side of the

Danska — the shady side — until I was presented with my truck-driver's disguise: turban, white robe, bug eye sunglasses, and the *de rigeur* apparel of all Chinese drivers, a pair of white gloves. After handshakes once more and farewell good wishes, Hai-yan hauled herself up into the seat beside me, I let out the clutch, and garlic and cabbages, Hai-yan and I rattled and rolled down the gravelly road on our way, we hoped, to Beijing.

We traveled about five kilometers, comrades, when we realized that the incredible heat we were feeling was not just from the Shanxi sun, but the fact that the heater in our Siberian transport could not be turned off. At least we could not figure out how to turn it off, or how to vent the hot air elsewhere than into our laps. I pulled to the roadside and looked over the wiring and the fusebox, but the only legible writing was in Russian and I was reluctant to start pulling plugs and cables for fear of disabling something crucial. Hai-yan told me I should have brought Mr. Whiz along. Of course we stripped to essentials (and that damned robe was too hot anyway) and used the now superfluous clothes to stuff the heater vents, a tactic that was only modestly successful, but at least kept us from being blasted by a continuous jet of heat.

We drove on, sweating copiously, our lips and tongues drying. We stopped now and then and fortified ourselves with *qi sue* and chunks of watermelon (though I didn't leave the cab) and were glad when at last night fell and we could undress completely, except for my turban, gloves, and shoes.

And so it came to pass, comrades, that I drove across Shanxi and Hebei provinces in the near buff with a nude woman by my side. Yes, there were erotic interludes — several, in fact. We dared a midnight swim in a broad irrigation canal, chased each other through a grove like satyr and nymph, fondled and fooled as we careened along the country roads of China. Lucky me! I thought. It was not the turban, after all, which provided my disguise, but the garlic and cabbages bouncing along behind. When it became light again, we dressed with the greatest reluctance, if not weariness also. How young she had made me feel all night! But now, as our journey reached its fourteenth hour and the heat of another day was approaching, I began to feel my age.

What an awful feeling it is to be falling asleep at the wheel! I battled that drowsiness for ten hours more, when the Beijing skyline provided the last adrenaline jolt to carry me through.

10

M*r. fisher, we have been perusing our maps of the Da Tong area, but can find no town or village named "Zuotian", which, we presume you know, means also "yesterday".*

Comrades, I only know what I was told. I thought I was in a town called Zuotian. Anyway, I'm sure it took us about four hours tractor ride from Datong to the northwest. I think northwest. No. Maybe southwest?

What route did you take out of this so-called Zuotian to return to Beijing?

The *only* route, comrades. There was only one main street that went anywhere.

Do you remember any particular landmarks, features of the countryside, or the like?

I told you that we began our journey in the evening out of rolling hills in a dry, gravelly countryside. Night soon followed. On the return, my most vivid memory is of the irrigation pond Hai-yan and I played in, the moon on the water, her laughter so free and playful. I saw something that night I will remember forever.

Yes?

It's rather personal.

Every detail is important, Mr. Fisher, as you have noted.

Well, in Hindu mythology there is this image, this symbol, called the Great Indra Screen. I read about it years ago and it stuck in my mind as an incredibly beautiful vision. The Indra Screen is made out of an infinitude of diamonds, and every diamond reflects the image of every other diamond, rather like mirrors reflecting each other and offering an infinity of images. You've all probably done that as kids, placed one mirror before another and then tried to peek down that infinite corridor of mirror in mirror in mirror. . . .

You light one candle before the Indra Screen, you see, and it is as if the world were blazing. I assume this is a metaphor for religious faith. Perhaps it was on my mind because I was driving when normally I would have been asleep, and so was dreaming while awake.

But Hai-yan and I were splashing each other with water in the moonlight, and every drop flying in its arc glistened with moonlight before it fell again to the surface and was absorbed in the whole; and when I held her wriggling against me, comrades, wet and cool, I could see the water beading on her skin, and each drop also held a perfect moon in it, like the iris in an eye. She was speckled with moons, moons dripped through her hair, too, comrades, and tumbled from the nipples of her breasts. I almost fainted from the intensity of this perception. I had never seen anything so beautiful, and naturally for me at that moment every detail was also erotically and hopelessly charged. This beautiful, unobtainable young woman, in my arms, shimmering with moons!

But can you remember any detail of the landscape which would help identify the route you took to Beijing?

Hai-yan read the road signs. I only turned where she said to turn. Meanwhile I was more interested in the landscape inside the cab than outside. I paid only as much attention to the road as I had to.

All right, then, tell us what happened when you returned to Beijing with the truck.

Well, comrades, we were greeted by Wen in the work unit parking area, and I immediately took some of the wind out of his sails, his enthusiasm for the truck and his laughter at my get-up, by jumping in his butt about the thousand dollars and the fact we were now saddled with a truckload of garlic and cabbages — which, by the way, were becoming fairly redolent in the heat. I'm sure that Hai-yan and I smelled like *galumpkis,* too, but the point I made to Wen was that because he had shortchanged the dealers we now had to make up the deficit by selling these vegetables, and selling them fast. He was not very forthcoming about where my money had gone, but indeed seemed repentant and agreed without question that the responsibility for selling the new goods was on his shoulders. In a way I think he was happy that a means had been found to get him out of his jam with the truck dealers, even if it did not — by a long shot — clear the slate with me. You could also see he was delighted with the truck, his imagination inflamed by its possibilities.

I may as well confess now, comrades, that the cabbage and garlic sales were quite successful (Wen made enough on the proceeds to pay off his debt, whether he did so or not) and for that reason they became a regular addition to our enterprises. At this point our little empire encompassed these businesses:

bicycles;
watermelons;
rape and tomatoes (I believe);
and cabbages and garlic.

In a few days we would expand our business one more notch when we began renting out our truck to an associate of Chen Tai-pan's, a guy who was making some extra bucks hauling drain pipes in the evening.

But first, of course, we celebrated the arrival of our great new and blue Russian workhorse. Mr. Whiz went over it with a fine tooth comb, and pronounced it a creature of no major ailments, but one which would also require monitoring and regular maintenance. Yes, he agreed to take on the mechanic's role — for a reasonable fee, as usual. His first chore was to turn off the heater, a task he accomplished by removing a couple of hoses.

Now Wen and Chen had been charged with finding a place to keep the truck when it was not in service and this is where we met to show it off and welcome its arrival. Not that Bu Kou Yao is easy to find! Taxi drivers profess never to have heard of it. Neighbors in the area deny its existence. *Residents* claim ignorance of its location. But with Wen's help we gathered there for what in America would be termed a tailgate party, the tailgate in this case being a pretty hefty one. We were having a great time together, making extravagant plans, rapping with the people of the neighborhood, including the matriarch of the area, one Dong Xidi, a lively, laughing old lass with the face of a withered apple and gaps between her teeth.

Only Ms. Cao seemed a little aloof from our celebration, perhaps — if it is not too vain of me to think so — because she was a little jealous of the adventure Hai-yan and I had shared (the details of which she would never imagine) in bringing the truck to Beijing. Or perhaps she was beginning to see the danger in our enthusiasm, that we were, so to speak, driving into dangerous territory. She became, as she sometimes could, even while she helped herself to the *jaozi* and beer, quite official, even a little sarcastic, which I quite correctly took as a note of warning.

Once when we had a chance to drift off together in the shadows of the *hutong*, I asked her why she was not happy.

"I hope we know what we're getting into," she said. Then she put her fingers between the buttons on my shirt. "I hope my own feelings are not leading me into big trouble."

I placed my hands on her shoulders and looked — through her glasses — into her eyes. "Are we getting a little desperate?"

"I hate your 'we'," she said, and spun away.

At once I repented my cuteness, and lack of response to her anxiety, because it was also true that I was bluffing: she was right, and I knew it, and I was likewise getting a little scared. Events seemed steadily to be gaining control; the horse we were riding was becoming the master, and a reckless one at that. As I returned to the truck, I saw that Dong Xidi had watched the exchange between Ms. Cao and me and that instead of turning away discreetly she gave me a sympathetic shake of the head. A little drunk anyway, I put my arm over her shoulder and said, "Well, Dong Xidi, tell me, please, everything I need to know about Chinese women."

She returned my embrace by putting one of her short arms around my waist and rudely squeezing my fanny.

"They are so kind, they will do anything for you," she said. "That is what makes them so dangerous if you are ungrateful."

Well, I laughed at that, comrades, but not because I didn't think it might be true. How much I had to learn!

What is "Bu Kou Yao", No Mouth Duck?

Comrades! I assumed you knew. For one thing, it's the kingdom of Dong Xidi, that's for sure. She runs the place. What it is, though, is just a parking lot basically, in the center of a *hutong* that runs behind the zoo, Dong Yuan Park. A little parking lot, but a controlled one. I guess the name comes from the shape of the *hutong*, like a duck's neck, and the fact that it's a dead end. The parking lot is controlled, comrades, because it's a business.

Let's face it. Owning a car or truck in Beijing is next to impossible because a) you've got to have the money to buy one in the first place, b) the license fee is exorbitant, and c) worst of all, most impossible of all, you have to be able to prove you have someplace to garage the thing. Logistically, of course, it makes perfect sense, since space is of such a premium and a wealth of privately-owned vehicles would make Beijing's *hutong*s impassable. This is reasonable. Automobiles occupy space, and space in a city like Beijing is worth more than gold. Housing a car takes up as much space as what the average family is allotted for eating and sleeping. You know this. Your regulations are fierce, but necessary.

On the other hand, comrades, if the only obstacle between you and owning a car is a place to keep it, and if I have a little space, but no car, well? Isn't this a condition made for, some would say "exploitation", others "opportunity". So you see, the neighborhood of Bu Kou Yao has entered into the business of renting parking space. That's all. Dong Xidi simply makes sure that private cars parking in Bu Kou Yao have paid the neighborhood fee and are not molested. Back in New York, you see, a little kid comes up to you when you park, and he says, "Watch your car, Mister?" It's blackmail. You don't pay him, he busts your windows. So you pay him. Bu Kou Yao is not like that. It has a truer spirit. There is no blackmail. You get what you pay for: space and a pair of watchful eyes, two valuable commodities anywhere! Besides, Dong Xidi knows all the potential troublemakers from when they were wearing slit pants.

Riding a Tiger

Please tell us more about Dong Xidi.

Comrades! I am utterly disgusted with myself for letting the name of Dong Xidi slip my lips and enter into this sordid record. If any harm comes to her because of my careless tongue, you will not have to kill me, I will do it myself. To my mind, she represents an utterly new dimension in female potential, though it may also be true that she is a Chinese type with many historical precedents. She is kind, yet shrewd, with a species of street smarts — *realpolitik* of the neighborhood, comrades! — loving, and yet capable of expressing her authority and power in genuinely cruel ways. She knows the meaning of generosity, and also the meaning of revenge. At once she is quite spontaneous and open, and yet she can also be calculating, treacherous and even merciless. Self-effacing, she is also incurably ambitious for herself and her family.

So I came to call her the Yin/Yang Woman, for she was a rolling synthesis of many seeming contradictions. Yes, a devoted communist, comrades, committed to socialist ideals, to sharing the wealth; yet she was also not above an occasional appeal to prayer and was quite confident she could do better on her own than as a cog in the socialist machine. None of that Lei Feng stuff for her. She is grateful for all the Communist Party has led China to accomplish, but she also sees — I know I should not tell you this! — the party as too conservative, even obstructionist. I would say her greatest virtue is her survivability, her loving gumption. She has caught a lot of hell and seen a lot of changes in her sixty-five? seventy? Beijing years!

Not that she is flawless. She liked the Russians, you know, and likes them still. She could not understand the rift between Mao and Kruschev. She had taken the trouble to learn Russian, you see, and had made numerous Russian friends during the years of cooperation, and then that skill not only became useless but regarded as a badge of shame. The only person she could speak it with now was her old friend Chen Tai-pan, whom she met during the Cultural Revolution when they were both rusticated to the north, to dig iron ore. Life is so logical in retrospect, isn't it? And so chancy minute by minute as we muddle through.

Dong Xidi, comrades, knows the history, lineage, personality and prospects of every soul in her neighborhood. She is the virtual mayor of Bu Kou Yao, and a true communist/capitalist.

These terms are contradictory. How can one be both a communist and a capitalist?

Not "contradictory", comrades, but "paradoxical". Dong Xidi shares profits with her neighbors, has no desire to enhance her own life at the expense of others. She told me she believes we all have a right to life's necessities, which includes for her education and transportation. And yet she is greedy for improvement and wants not to be hindered from finding her own way to do this. She kills me. You know what she wants to do when she gets rich? She wants to open Beijing's first miniature golf course. Really! She read about miniature golf in some American magazine that she once came across and she would like to create a course with Chinese themes — the Dragon Hole, the Tiger Hole, the Pagoda Hole, etc.

How many cars were parked in Bu Kou Yao?

It's a small area, as I said. As few as four. As many as twelve.

Are all legally registered?

Don't be silly.

Could fire trucks, police cars or emergency vehicles make their way into Bu Kou Yao, sufficiently to perform the necessary duties?

Comrades! With greatest respect for your police and fire fighters, your emergency crews and public servants, the Bu Kou Yao does not represent a traffic or safety hazard to the community. The police are not as effective there as the people themselves, in preventing and correcting criminal acts, even the inevitable domestic wrangle. Everyone minds everybody's business. If you want to draw a crowd, all you have to do is start an argument in public. Try to rob somebody there and sixteen neighbors will be dragging you off by your heels. The police there are almost superfluous, and that may be also one benign result of your industrial limitations — not every jerk with a bad attitude has a pistol in his pocket. People are not afraid to step in.

As for fire fighting: the neighborhood is a complete and utter firetrap and if the Boston Fire Department were housed adjacent it could not guarantee for a minute that, given the outbreak of fire, every home in the area would not be glowing ash in half an hour. Another way of saying this, I suppose, is that Bu Kou Yao is a self-policing firetrap.

What are these privately-owned vehicles used for?

For transportation.

Yes, but whom or what is being transported?

I really don't know that. I didn't think it was a wise question to ask any of the car owners.

Are many of the car owners money-changers from western China?

Pardon me, comrades, but I lack the experience to make a clear distinction between a Han and a Mongol. I can identify individuals, but lack the sophistication to identify regional differences among you. And why else did the Manchus require pigtails on their vassals? I know you

Riding a Tiger

take these differences very seriously, but I have to wonder if they're all they're cracked up to be.
Was there any indication these unregistered vehicles were used for illegal activity?
Not that I was aware. Of course driving an unregistered car is an illegal activity.
Besides driving we mean.
One fellow lived in his car, a kind of van. At least he slept in it.
So you regularly parked your truck in Bu Kou Yao, and conducted other business there, such as truck leasing?
Yes.
Did anyone in the neighborhood question this activity?
Everyone questioned us. They all wanted to know what we were doing.
And what did you tell them?
That we were selling surplus melons and renting trucks.
Did no one question your honesty?
Not to our faces. Did anyone report us?
You mentioned Ms. Cao's "jealousy" at the beginning of this chapter. In reviewing your self-criticism we also see you have avoided our question regarding the exact nature of your relationship to her. We want a full accounting. We want the whole truth.

You want the truth? The truth, no less! You assume I know what it is, and can tell it. The truth, or a version of the truth, comrades?

Perhaps she was a spy? Any chance, comrades, that she was encouraged to win my heart and steal all my computer secrets, copy all my Apple, Digital, and IBM compatible diskettes?

No, that does not have the ring of truth to it. If you told me this and showed me documents, I would probably never believe it. I would not be able to believe it, and live. Maybe it's the personal level of what Krazy Kirby is always going on about: what we don't face because we can't, even our very own creations!

Is it the truth that Cao Song-wen eventually took off her clothes and lay beside me? Do you think that the nipples of her breasts passed between my lips, or that she groaned with pleasure beneath my middle-aged, white Western belly?

You are aware, I presume, that among Westerners, Chinese women are considered to be small-breasted. It was a common topic among the UNB, I assure you. Many men in Western culture, and a few foolish women, too, equate femininity and sexual attractiveness with the size of a woman's breasts. This is a cultural difference of some import in this case. How do you know that I did not find Cao Song-wen boyish and unattractive? Besides being small-breasted, she had heavy and dark eyebrows, which in Aryan culture are taken to be signs of masculinity, unattractive in women, and all sorts of depilating tools are available on the Western markets to offer proof of this. Her eyes, like your eyes, are narrow, and narrowed eyes in the Western world suggest evasiveness, untrustworthiness. About her lips, there was no question. Not as full as Hai-yan's, they were nevertheless exquisite. I'm sure that you found them too full, perhaps even a little obscene, and Song-wen would hold her mouth pinched sometimes, to diminish what she mistakenly took to be the unattractiveness of her mouth. I can confess to you that I did admire those lips, but I am asking you also to consider whether these alone could have turned me into a monster of lust.

These lines, you remonstrate, have little to do with the matter of the correctness of your actions.

But you assume I am guilty! And whatever I did or did not do, I still say to you that the important question has nothing much to do with correctness or even morality of my choices and Song-wen's complicity in them, but their very reality, whether we could even see it, and bear it.

Comrades! I meant to say to you long ago, in three pages, yes, I have done as you charged, and, yes, I agree that my conduct was decadent and bourgeois. I have since learned how to behave properly and accept the discipline of the Party and am grateful to it for this opportunity to become a more responsible participant in building China's four modernizations. Then I intended to lay out an objective chronology of events establishing my seduction of an innocent young comrade.

But there is no "objective" chronology of events.

There is nothing objective about seduction, and the seduction may have been a lie, or it may have been double-sided, or "seduction" may be entirely inappropriate. Or perhaps she seduced me by pretending that I could seduce her.

What is "innocent", in this connection?

What is "young", for that matter?

What is "comrade"?

Every word in this testament, which is as honest as I can make it, glows with unreliability, with deceptions and tricks. But they may also be true.

Comrades! Suppose I put it this way:

I, Arnold Fisher, a Caucasian male of 45 years of age, American, did insert my erect penis, covered by a Chinese prophylactic of "large" size (not bragging, comrades, since I believe your condom control unit

Riding a Tiger

exercises the same sort of sizing standards as American soap packagers — economy, large, and giant) into the vagina of Cao Song-wen, a Chinese female of thirty or more years in my hotel rooms and elsewhere on several occasions.

Well?

You see immediately how unsatisfactory such a report is. Would it, for example, be of interest to know that on one occasion the alleged union lasted only thirty-three seconds owing to an inopportune phone call? That on another occasion, the union lasted more than two hours? And what are these "facts" but brutal distortions of the experience?

What of the word "insert"?

What is the linguistic implication of mentioning myself before I mention Cao Song-wen?

What does it mean to say that I am an American, or Cao Song-wen a Chinese woman of so many years? This might not even establish our races.

Does it mean I am a Christian?

Does it mean I voted for Ronald Reagan?

Does it mean I am rich?

Does it mean I am racist?

We could make up an interesting little test for computer analysis, a chart of responses by Chinese to the word "American", and vice versa, and the results might tell us how ready we are to see the Other. I held her in my arms, comrades, and I looked into her eyes. But Who, What did I see?

All these descriptions of all these events lack essential qualities. The events themselves are nothing, but cannot even be described in a meaningful way, if I cannot count on you to have a similarity of mind, and expectation, and method. What did I think I was doing? What did Song-wen imagine to be taking place? And you, comrades, what do you presume?

I think I can venture this much with certainty, comrades: the relationship between Cao Song-wen and myself transcended cultural exchange.

Comrades! I beg you, do not be insulted. I respect your authority, the right to impose on me this duty to explain myself. It will make a great deal of difference to the living, I'm sure. It will settle all our stomachs. I'm sure I can justify everything, that we can all save face.

All of us except Chen Tai-pan.

You are entirely right. We must find answers. I am happy to take the blame.

II

THESE PROCEEDINGS *are not very orderly. We think you should spend a little more time to organize your thoughts and present them more efficiently.*
Comrades, this is not a true question. Also you must understand that part of my mission here has been to explain a very serious dichotomy between — well, it amounts to a "gap", as we say in America, between the generations. You see, linear thinking, literary culture, is dead. The future belongs to those of us who, brains imprinted by television cartoons, advertising, documentaries, live reports, are less strategic in our outlook and more — well — *jazzy!* I mean, "spontaneous". Also the computer, you see, which I represent (I mean I am a cultural representative of the computer generation), is intensely logical and rigorous at the basic level, but very free form, very "plastic", as we say, ideally. All due respect, comrades, but you sound *exactly,* I mean *exactly* like my Freshman English teacher! What we have here, I believe, is a foretaste of another gap, between developed and undeveloped countries. Here you are struggling for literacy, and the developed world is struggling for computer literacy. I mean, *how* are we going to communicate?

I guess it's not entirely true that we aren't *strategic,* as I said. Computers are strategic, but not linear. Omigod, what am I getting into here? The Chinese — wouldn't you agree, comrades? — love chess. Well, the computer is chess, but like three dimensional chess. Right! It's one more dimension, but that new dimension raises the stakes, and the potentialities by another factor — like ten to the third power instead of ten squared. So! These proceedings may at first seem chaotic, but comrades! Trust me. I did not get to be an enemy of the state through a disorganized mind!

We are also tired of being mocked, Mr. Fisher. Let us remind you that several of your colleagues in these unauthorized businesses have also been detained, in less comfortable circumstances, and their punishment and rehabilitation is intimately linked to what we learn from you. We have asked about Ms. Cao not to invade your privacy as you seem to think, but for sound political reasons. We are persuaded, for example, that awareness of your sexual duplicity will affect the understanding of both Ms. Cao and Tai Hai-yan about the nature of their relationship to you, to each other, and the enterprises they shared with you. The exact nature of your sexual behavior may also have importance in our investigation of Chen Tai-pan's murder.

Riding a Tiger

I see.
Perhaps you would like to begin again with Ms. Cao.
Yes. Let me think about it.
Tonight you will write this.
Yes.
I can't imagine how I am going to make myself understood. But knowing who I am going to hurt at least makes composing this document easier.

Is there something wrong with me, comrades, if I do not feel like a criminal? What would I change, if I had it to do over again?

I think it is possible to love three women at once, especially if you are not living with any of them.

I think the need for duplicity (or triplicity) is tragic, but is there a society in which it is not necessary? Or at least a lesser evil?

You will recall that I am married. On this basis alone, it was never a matter of simply juggling girl-friends, but of considered choice, and risk, and need. And love! Can you truly feel, after reading this testament so far, that I have treated these women as courtesans?

Not only did I think of my own wife, comrades, I thought of Ms. Cao's husband, how he might suffer if he learned his wife was bedding with a foreign expert; and I thought of Hai-yan's future husband, who might not be gratified after all to find his bride was unexpectedly sexually sophisticated, ask himself (or her) some painful questions, and disturb the peace between them. And yet I state here and now unequivocally: I love my wife; I love Cao Song-wen; I love Tai Hai-yan. Furthermore, I never lied about my wife to my Chinese lovers, who knew our connection was temporary, even as I knew and understood my relations with Hai-yan were in one way hopeless, and with Song-wen doomed. Further still, after twenty years of marriage, although I expect discretion and fair warning if our marriage is in danger, I expect behavior from my wife no different from my own. I did not demand or expect anything from Ms. Cao that would compromise her marriage: she chose if, when and where to join me. And I have testified already that between Hai-yan and me, her word was law.

Comrades! How can I make sense to you? In the West we emphasize "individualism" so much and have thus become so preoccupied with "alienation", we sometimes forget we can, and often do, become different people in different relationships. The Other helps us to realize potentials that by ourselves we might never know existed. I sometimes even think we would have no cause to hate at all if we didn't see in the people we despise a frightening potential of our own. Why else would we even notice such people? Between those we hate and those we love is a vast sea of beings who barely graze our consciousness. Is it then possible that something in our psyche responds more attentively to those we love and hate, out of a similar necessity?

I suppose it goes without saying, comrades, that after twenty years of marriage my wife and I have experienced many sides of each other, but I am also sure there are corners we keep private, perhaps for dignity's sake, perhaps also not to cause each other unnecessary pain — as we judge it. I have seen things, by accident, I know my wife would prefer to keep to herself, and so I pretend never to have seen them. I have heard from her friends, and overheard things, that I have pretended not to have heard. At my age I know perfectly well that no one person can be all things and all people to another; we make our commitments, but we do not live in a vacuum.

Perhaps more trouble enters a relationship the higher the expectations are. Not that they shouldn't be reasonably high, after all, or that anyone's goal should be to live a trouble-free life. A marriage may be quite comfortable and comforting, as I believe mine is, but it should never become a prison! What marriage can maintain a perpetual springtime? Show me a marriage without changes, without new pleasures and risks entering into it, without adventure, and comrades, I will show you opium, or a corpse.

People find it odd, I've learned, that Americans have made "the pursuit of happiness" a testament of faith, a declared right, an institution, a reasonable goal for all its citizens. Any grand abstraction might have been substituted for the famous one — "truth", "wisdom", "success"....
"*All men are created equal, endowed with certain inalienable rights, among them life, liberty, and the pursuit of profit.*" Comrades! I have just committed blasphemy. But does it make a point?

Is not America, the Land of the Free, also the Land of the Happy? Is the railroad porter happy? Is the prosecuting attorney happy? How about the very President and the First Lady: were they not recently photographed dancing in the reflected radiance of political successes — money for this missile and those freedom fighters, etc. etc. What a happy time! Everyone rich and safe and living at least ten miles from ground zero?

If you take one of those channel-changers, comrades, and sit in front of a suitably equipped American television, and rapidly spin through the offerings, you will see nothing but happiness: false teeth that stay in place, instant pain relief, flowing hair, firm tits, shining metal, gleaming plastic, slicers and dicers that perform miracles, and every customer, every user and abuser smiling to beat the band. White teeth! Healthier gums! A low-fat, fiber-rich, and extra calcium existence! All the pleasure, comrades, in our America, and none of the calories, or beatings, jailings, thefts, and certainly no thermonuclear anxiety. We pursue happiness the way the dogs pursue the fox, and when we catch it, comrades, what bloody fun!

Now, please, don't ask me to explain why the pursuit of happiness is a right and almost all forms of pleasure are regarded as sins. Who's defining happiness here? I don't think it's Thomas Jefferson! Happiness is a microwave. A refrigerator. Sex in the back seat of a shiny car. We pursue it. We invent it. We even think we know what it is!

Now, then, if I have been a more than usually civilized fellow, a harder worker, and a man with more conscience than I might otherwise display with others in relation to my wife, I think I have also explained what I liked about myself in relation to Hai-yan: I discovered with her new realms of patience and gentleness, spontaneity and passion, among other things.

But now you ask me to focus on Ms. Cao, dear Song-wen the practical and tactful one, the political one, Song-wen of the cloistering, retrograde, decomposing marriage, Song-wen who was afraid of the love she felt because it always seemed to come back spoiled, even afraid of her freedom — a factor everywhere, comrades, even in the USA. Dogma is so comforting! In love, or in politics. And she was jealous! You see, I didn't think enough of myself to think this was even possible.

She had another dimension, comrades, which took me by surprise, given her otherwise total sophistication, and given the very pleasant, if blurry, first sexual encounter, which I've already described. On that basis, you see, I made assumptions about her sexual knowledge and practice that I had soon to revise, and radically.

It's possible, though neither of us were virgin, that we were in the originality of our coming together, a bit like Adam and Eve. That first coupling was so unconscious, so natural, that we only knew we wanted more of it. But when we grew aware of this marvelous fact, and began to will our encounter to be what we hoped and expected — trouble. Was it July or August that I am thinking of? It was before the second gondola and long before Chen Tai-pan was found dead. I know it was a hot afternoon and we arrived at the hotel in a lather, and also a little nervous and excited. We had plenty of time and had picked an afternoon and evening free of other events. So there we were. We picked our sticky clothes off each other and took a shower together — something which would be very difficult, even unpleasant in the Chinese-style bathrooms I have seen, the squat toilet between your feet. Song-wen was very shy and modest and we behaved in the shower as if we were strangers at a tea. I found this touching, frankly, but there was no possibility of my treating her like an animal. She set the tempo, and I was happy to dance to it.

As soon as we were in the bedroom, however, Song-wen sat on the edge of the bed, declared "now is the time for sex," grabbed my — we have, as you do, comrades, many words for *penis,* which sounds rather medical, and each with its own connotations, most of them brutal, but for reasons soon to become apparent, I am going to choose the word — tool, and began pumping it so vigorously that it appeared to me to be an attack. She continued this — painful! — activity even as she fell back on the bed, legs apart, as if she expected me to plunge upon her. Her eyes were shut tight, her face turned aside as if she were expecting a blow.

Needless to say — or is it? — I did not rise to the occasion. Our tradesmen have a sophisticated array of tools available to them, and they are fond of saying that the way to solve the problems of their craft is to choose "the right tool for the right job". I say this because this beautiful, mature woman, her long, black hair curling at the nipples of her breasts, was rummaging in my crotch like a carpenter pawing through a toolbox for the right drill bit or file.

Comrades, her aggressiveness not only took me by surprise, but I think it is fair to say also, put me in a state of shock. I might have dealt with it all readily and happily if I had ever caught even the slightest tendency in Song-wen's personality to alert me to this potential. But to me it seemed all too willful, even violent, far more athletic than erotic, too mechanical and determined. I tried, in vain, to be accommodating, to join the spirit of her efforts, but it was just plain painful to me, clamped in her vice-grips, and Song-wen herself seemed too desperate for quick results to be enjoying herself even the slightest bit.

"I knew it," she said, collapsing and rolling away. "You don't love me."

I lay next to her now, her buttocks in my lap. "Don't be silly," I said. "You're immensely attractive to me. Haven't I shown you already? I just need a little more time, and you don't need to try so hard."

"I knew it," she said. "I'm no good at this."

"Hey!" I said. "We're humans. We have to learn everything."

She seemed to collapse further into despair now. Gently, I slid my hand under her arm and began to stroke her breast.

"I don't know what to do," she said.
"I do," I said. "I'll show you."

And I did, comrades, I showed her many things, many things about herself as well as about males, and by the end of the afternoon, we were both well satisfied. As we lay in each other's arms, talking, Song-wen confided what her sex life had been like for the last six years. If and when her husband wanted to fuck — "make love" dignifies it — he would wait for Song-wen in the bed, mount her, already hard, as soon as she slipped beneath the covers, then finish the operation quickly. Most of the time, she said, she never even became reasonably moist, and she had not known it was even the expected and the right thing to happen.

"Most Chinese women," she told me, "say sex is 'man's business'. They endure it because they want to have children, or because they believe it is just something a man must do."

"But haven't you read about sex at all?"

"China is too puritanical," she said. "We learn about birth control, but not pleasure. I have seen a book on sexual hygiene. Anything else is forbidden."

"Poor China," I said.

"Maybe it's one reason why people want to go abroad." She laughed as she said this.

"In America, did you have a lover?"

"No," she said, a little in a pet. "I was too shy."

"You didn't read any American books on sex?"

"I was too shy to ask for them. But I also was too busy with other things. I didn't think about it that much."

"But my dear Song-wen," I said. "You have a right to pleasure, especially at your age."

"It's such a luxury!" she said, scanning the room. "A bed like this. Shower. Heated in the winter. Privacy. All these things are unusual for us. I wonder if it is true that most Chinese make love most of the time with most of their clothes on?"

"Surely you exaggerate," I laughed.

"I'm not sure."

"We could make a survey," I said, "put it on the computer."

"No one will talk about it truthfully, if at all," she said. "Your data will be junk."

"I wish I had a good book on sex for you," I said.

She kissed me. "You're better than a book. You'll teach me many more things, won't you?"

"Yes," I said. "I'll teach you one right now." I kissed my way down the length of her torso, my *dim sum*, and lingered in that place there are so many words for, until she gave a cry and trembled, and called my name, her fingers knotted in the little hair I have.

Comrades! As befits an industrial society, our lexicon for *penis* includes the following: tool, hammer, daub, rod, pile-driver, drill, shaft, piston, prick and plunger, among others; the sexual act itself is sometimes called a "screw" or "screwing", sometimes "pumping", sometimes even "planking", which may be the oddest locution of all. I'm sure that in a short while computer terminology will also be applied.

As for Song-wen and I, we rid our relationship of the brutal and the hurried, as much as possible. I never took her in anger or frustration, as I have done, on rare and by now historical occasions, even with my own wife.

"First," I told her, "I think we should find out what you like, what makes you feel good. After that I will tell you what I like and you can tell me if you like to do them."

"Very systematic," she said.

"Pure science," I replied. "It's the fifth modernization."

She laughed and laughed at that, a rare treat to see.

Comrades! I am not attempting blasphemy when I raise these questions, but am genuinely concerned: what, do you suppose, was the sex life of poor, carbuncled Karl Marx?

Of Lenin?

Could a man like Stalin ever have fallen in love?

Even Hitler had a girl-friend, the devoted Eva Braun. What, behind closed doors, could possibly have transpired? How can we imagine anything but Sadean acts, boots, whips, chains? Was he capable of even the minutest tenderness? Seeing him with his pants down, could she really believe him a Superman, imagine him ruler of the world?

The fifth modernization, comrades. That is what Song-wen and I explored: happy, gentle, prolonged sex. I assume it will have political consequences.

12

COMRADES, I AM NOT FEELING WELL TONIGHT. I am feeling a little sad, very much missing my wife and daughter. Something is happening to me, apparently, that is so profound I can't even name it, say what the "problem" is. I have been over every square inch of this suite, the two rooms and the bathroom, and this palatial prison tonight seems immensely tiresome and tawdry and limiting. I knew something was wrong the minute I killed a rather fat cockroach in the bathroom — two swats were required — and immediately felt this terrible, all-encompassing remorse.

I scooped up the roach (no respecter of borders or oceans, this species) in a piece of paper and gave him a regular funeral — I mean it — complete with prayers and hymns, whatever I could remember of such ceremonies from my youth. The death of this roach seemed immense and sad to me — still does — and in psychological terms, I suppose I am "projecting", seeing myself in the roach, realizing the reality of my own potentially quite imminent demise.

I am thinking also of Chen Tai-pan, and the fact I was not able to see him laid to rest, or participate in that, and so perhaps for me the roach funeral is a little ceremony of closure, filling in, making an ending. Jesus Christ, I admired him! What a hell of a man he was, in my view. Was he a father-figure to me, at my age, myself a father? It is possible. Possible, hell. It's true!

So the death of this stupid roach which I whacked with a wet towel has devastated me. Insects! I hate them. And yet I know how necessary they are, part of the wave of life forms.

I am thinking now of the night Chen came to play the piano as usual, an abbreviated practice, and later, as we walked in a misting rain to the bus stop, his pulling me into the comparative shelter of the shed from which Hai-yan and Mr. Whiz were liberating bicycles, and remarking "What is going on out west? With the people who sold the truck?"

"I don't know anything about it," I said. "Once in a while somebody Wen hired goes out for a load of cabbage and garlic. What's the problem?"

"I'm getting the sense that people out there feel they are being shortchanged."

"It's all Wen's family, isn't it?"

"Family so-called."

"Why do you say this? I met Wen's cousin. I went to the commune."

"All the same," Chen said. "I'm hearing some ugly rumors."

"Such as?"

"Wen seems to be looking out for himself. How strict are your accounts?"

"Not very."

"Maybe in Wen's case you should create some books. How good is your memory?"

"Very good," I said. "When it comes to loans and investments I am a natural calculator."

Chen laughed easily. "I laugh not because this is a laughing matter — far from it. But because it is apparent to me how suited some minds are for certain tasks. Some mathematical, musical. Some linguistic. Some spatial. Some — I don't know a good word for it — insightful about people, about feelings."

I asked him how he would categorize me.

He shrugged, faced me with an expression I thought painful. "Oh, I don't know," he said. "I've thought at times you were a misplaced musician."

"Really?"

"Yes."

"But, Chen, I can't carry a tune in a bathtub."

He replied readily, smiling. "And I am not a great judge of people. But I do think Wen bears, as you say, calling on the carpet?"

"Thank you," I said.

He smiled again, an eerie smile, now that I think of it. So quick! He left me pondering what I might have been like as a musician, but I didn't see much sense in that. Maybe a blues singer? The connections he made on the basis of what he knew of me were too elusive to reconstruct. His was a mind I really couldn't know — but I could admire it!

I didn't have to follow Chen's advice and corner Wen because a few nights later, quite late, in fact, as I was brushing my teeth with my first dose of Chinese toothpaste (my tube of Crest had finally expired) and wondering if it were a mixture of sand and jelly, Wen was at my door! I let him in and, in my pajamas, finished preparing for bed before I talked to him.

"Can I stay for the night?" he asked.

"Sure," I said. "Trouble?"

"Trouble at home," he said.

Since I had an extra bed and Wen was going to taxi me to work in the morning, it was not a great inconvenience to me, would only surprise the hotel make-up crews when they had two beds to deal with instead of one. But I was also merciless:

"Listen," I said. "I'm hearing you've got problems out west. What's the story?"

He did not, or pretended not to understand these allusions, so I rephrased them.

"Look, you got trouble with your family? You owe somebody money?"

"Agh! These country people," he said, waving the question away. "It's not serious. Relatives are always complaining about something."

This was the best I could do. He was quickly out of his clothes and soon snoring tremendously. Wen, I thought as I fell sleep, was the first person I had ever seen who looked larger, should I say "fatter"? lying down. And what a rumble from that little nose of his. One can make too much of the differences between the races.

With all these clues assaulting me, comrades, you would think I would have been more terrified than ever. But no. I was quite as oblivious then to the machinations of the Fates as I am right now. Some things do not improve with age. In the morning, over tea at the experts' dining hall, Wen revealed that the second gondola of melons was on its way. Once again the timing, for me, was terrifically inconvenient.

I literally pounded the table, like a Soviet boss. "But goddammit, that's the night I'm supposed to be in Ba Da Ling, with some people running the tourist stores, inventory questions. I won't be back until. . . ."

"I know," Wen said. "Midnight. Remember? I driving you."

"Oh, right."

"I think it's good timing," Wen said.

"What about the truck? Don't tell me it's rented."

"No problem," Wen said, smiling.

"Then we'd better call the troops," I said. "Hell Night number two."

"Better this time," Wen said.

"I'll believe it when I see it," I said. The thought of hassling all those melons made me instantly tired.

"Call that guy, too," Wen said.

I knew whom he meant, and I mulled it over, but decided against it. For my part, I was happy to be done with Kirby forever.

Well, comrades, what Wen said was true, and sometimes we do get what we ask for in life, and it is good, even though it is not everything we want as well. In this case, Kirby showed up again, grinning, maniacally ready to throw melons. But this time, too, thanks to Mr. Whiz and the truck, the whole enterprise was much less arduous, and altogether more efficient and successful.

I will not go into detail on unloading gondola number two, except to say that Mr. Whiz, between bicycles, had created two "slides" out of metal pipe and bamboo webbing that reached from the gondola to the wall, and to the truck from the wall, so that it was only necessary to lift the melons onto this slide and watch them roll by grace of gravity slowly to the truck where the major task there was simply to stack them in the most space-conserving order. I think Kirby was even a little disappointed and bored because we had achieved such mechanized success — or perhaps, being an engineer of sorts, he was a trifle jealous of Mr. Whiz's solution to our watermelon transport problems. He left us, Kirby did, early, grumbling about something we were too busy to bother trying to understand.

The truck ran beautifully. Unloading the gondola took precisely two hours and fifty-six minutes and ten truckloads of melons, the last load being a small one, and each run to and from the unloading yard only eighteen minutes!

I took Mr. Whiz under my arm and punched him playfully in the gut. He laughed and in reply presented me with a bill for labor and materials for making the slides for damn near 250 *kuai!* I rocked, but I remembered the hundreds of melons we had lost on the last outing, I rocked and I paid. I'd make it back in one truckload of sales.

"You little son-of-a-bitch!" I said, giving him a Dutch rub, which only made him laugh.

He still didn't know a word of English, and I still couldn't pronounce his name, but comrades! it was a joyous morning. I took the crew to breakfast Western-style at the Xiyuan Hotel and if the staff was consternated at our invasion, we made ourselves welcome by handing out melons galore. The chef even came out and sat down with us.

Oh, comrades, you know how these things go. In the course of conversation I somehow agreed to send him, from America, a couple dozen apprentice cooks who could learn from him the subtleties of Chinese cooking — for a fee, of course — and also take off his hands this hateful chore of making toast and frying, boiling, poaching eggs to please the Westerners. He begged me — I'm not kidding — for a good, cheap jam that would satisfy both Texan and Englishman, and comrades! if I ever get out of here, I'm going to look into it. God only knows what somebody would pay for maple syrup 12,500 miles from Burlington, Vermont or Hartford, Connecticut. Should we consider — I ask this in the spirit of fulfilling the worthy mission of reforesting China — importing sugar maple trees?

Comrades!

I know a guy, I think, who could supply bushels of seeds or seedlings. Whichever.

Cheap!

13

AFTER THE SECOND GONDOLA of melons was on the streets, comrades, the money came rolling in. Even splitting it six or seven ways, we were swimming in dough. My investment was quickly paid back, not in the same FEC or US dollars I had laid out, but in *renminbi*. I was storing it everywhere — in my suit coat pockets, under the television, under the what do you call 'ems, those stand up clothes chests you see in every Chinese room. (And that's another thing. Why the hell can't you people build a room with closets in it? These damned toe-stubbers and elbow-whackers are everywhere! You assign people two square meters apiece and then expect them to stuff into it one of these monstrosities.)

"What you going to do?" Hai-yan asked me one day. "You can't take away Chinese *kuai?*"

"No, I can't," I said. "I've got to find some way to change the stuff into American dollars, or European currency, or *yen.*"

"You change money?"

"I could, but that takes time I haven't got, and I don't want to get in trouble with the Mongolians already in the biz. Besides, if I did it, I'd be losing about twenty per cent."

"Maybe," she said, "you better sell something to foreign expert, tourists, somebody like that."

I looked at her closely, suddenly certain this was not an innocent remark. "O.K.," I said, *"who* do you know who has *what* to sell?"

"My sister has chickens."

"Chickens."

"Not live chickens. I mean cooked, very special. We call it 'Golden Chicken.'"

"Can I taste it?"

"Sure!"

"When?"

"I call my sister. I tell you."

"There's the phone."

"You give her *renminbi,* she buys chickens, cooks them. But takes two, three days, because she puts chicken in sauce a long time."

"Marinate."

"What is?"

"That's the word we use when you soak meat in a sauce. Marinate."

Riding a Tiger

"Ah!" She whipped out her ever-present notebook. "Please, you write this word."

As I wrote in the notebook I asked Hai-yan how long she and her sister had been plotting to sell boxed roasted chickens to foreign experts.

"We think of this a long time ago," she said. "But never have money."

"You may not be allowed on the hotel grounds, you know. Then what?"

"We buy tricycle. We sell at bus stop. Foreign expert can walk there."

You see, comrades, the instant this idea was mentioned to me, I knew at once it would work. Nothing would delight the UNB more than catered gourmet chicken, especially if it could be delivered to their rooms.

"We've got to find a way to make delivery," I insisted. "These foreigners love service like that. To go to the bus stop you have to put on your shoes and maybe it's raining and they don't want to go out or they're writing a report and don't want to interrupt the train of thought, or they're sick, or there's a volleyball game on TV and they don't want to miss any action."

"Train of thought?" she asked.

I explained this.

"Maybe we can hire expert, bring chicken in."

"There's several teenagers around. I think my friend Edith has a couple of kids who might like a little job like that."

"Please to find out!"

"Right away, boss. First, I want to taste this 'Golden Chicken.'"

"My sister bring some tonight."

"I'm so surprised."

Comrades! Golden Chicken was … is … not just delicious, but delicious to the point that you become quiet and introspective, a little stupefied with gratification, and sit there quite happily licking your fingers. There was absolutely no question that we could sell this chicken, and I knew instantly that once the UNB and others at the You Yi got a taste of it, Golden Chicken would become a requirement in their lives — in retail terms only, kind of the pizza of Beijing. Therefore, I suggested a promotional supper or box-lunch give-away, just a small sample to incite the demand I knew that this delicious dish would spark.

Now Hai-yan's sister, comrades, spoke no English, and though she is four or five years older and the mother of a demanding, chubby, curious, energetic little emperor (what will China become when this generation of spoiled brats hits the scene?) she is as beautiful and as seemingly unspoiled and fresh as her virginal sister. And spunky! I know women hate to be called "spunky" — or "feisty", even worse — but it's a damned good word, it fits Hai-yan's sister to a "T", and it does not demean her in the least. (This PR appropriation of words galls me. I have nothing against homosexuality, but I'm outraged at the appropriation of the word "gay", a very useful and necessary word which you cannot now use without conjuring up someone's sexual preference. Or take the word "real". What's real? Ke Kou Ke Le is real, an incredible inversion of reality. When accounts are written about the decline of the West, one of the priority topics must surely be the sapping of its language, language abuse, and the subsequent lopping off of whole important realms of feeling and potential and connection to . . . oh oh! . . . the real.)

I could see at once, that is, that Hai-yan's sister was the kind of person who would not be flustered if the action got hot and heavy, as it always does in the food business; she also was clearly the kind of person who could do several things at once, like any good short order cook or basketball star. She truly made me regret not being able to understand more Chinese than I did, because the exchanges between her and Hai-yan were crackling, and I could see they were both excited about the prospects of this new undertaking. Could she make bread? I asked. *Mien bao?* Oh yes, good bread. Could she put together Golden Chicken with the bread and a little extra sauce in an easily portable box? No problem! they declared. So Golden Chicken was launched.

Like a rocket.

Remember Edith, comrades, who first saw that Krazy Kirby should be exported to Canada for the sake of his mental health, the safety of the UNB, and the good of China? As I mentioned, she had several children, including a teenage brother and sister continuously at loggerheads and, unhappy with the difficulties of their Chinese school, frequent class-cutters. They would skip school and then hang around the You Yi apparently with no better purpose in mind than to torture each other with insults and accusations. All too frequently we overheard their skirmishes in the dining room. Well, I hired them. That is, Golden Chicken hired them. I'm not proud to say, comrades, that I could see in this situation of intense sibling rivalry the fuel for some aggressive salesmanship. On the other hand, I suppose it is also true that I gave some focus to their jealousies and a concrete way for them to play out their need for attention and a sense of worth. Other kids sell newspapers; these kids were going to sell Golden Chicken.

And sell it they did! Dear God! I had faith that the business would do well, but no real concept of how very, very well. It quite readily overwhelmed the facilities that Hai-yan's sister had to work in — the little three-by-nine foot kitchen with its two-burner propane stove and the "roaster" she had built atop this (and had to dismantle every time she had to cook for her own family.) The demand for Golden Chicken which Edith's two young hustlers drummed up beset us with some awful problems.

The most paramount was the need for another refrigerator. Now Hai-yan's sister already had one, but as you know, comrades, a refrigerator is considered a great luxury and owning two would be something of an affront to the community. Therefore, we not only had to buy a second refrigerator for the business, we had to smuggle it into her apartment, *and* find a way to conceal it there. Another midnight operation.

No one could think of these things if they did not happen to them. But this is China: of course we could use our own truck to haul the refrigerator to the apartment complex, but the entrance to the compound is scaled for only pedestrians and bicycles, the assumption being that no one has a car or that the buildings will never catch fire. If in fact there is a fire approach lane, we couldn't find it, or the gate to it was locked for protection against thieves. You Chinese are great believers in sealed-off living areas, a very traditional and comforting notion, to be sure, but one which now required us to lug a refrigerator about a quarter of a mile over a brick walk. By "we" I mean Hai-yan and her sister, brother-in-law (a wiry little rascal with a continuous nervous laugh and a perpetual cigarette) and me.

By the time we had hassled the refrigerator down the walk, it was another case of wondering if it was time for my first heart attack, whether I was going to end my life hauling a refrigerator at midnight for Golden Chicken Enterprises because the neighbors would be outraged by any-one's owning two such luxuries. Perhaps most deaths are equally absurd. How few of us get a chance to be a Joan of Arc or Alamo hero or revolutionary martyr. The night was so humid you could see no stars above and even breathing was hard. But we recouped and forged ahead.

The Fates had decreed our Sisyphean punishment to be that Hai-yan's sister lived on the sixth floor. They also decreed, as happens frequently in your power-scarce country, the electrical service had been shut off until morning and the hallways and stairways were pitch dark. I mean dark-room dark. So dark I saw nothing but purple flashes now and then — the futile exercising of rods and cones within my own eye.

In addition, space requirements being what they are in any Chinese apartment complex, the stairwells, landings and hallways are cluttered with all the excess gear that cannot be stored within the apartments themselves. Bicycles are lashed to the railings; houseplants and boxes of cooking utensils, odd piles of lumber, laundry, children's toys and bird cages and extra furniture accumulate everywhere — the kind of stuff that clutters the American garage, or attic, or basement. It is difficult enough to negotiate these passageways in daylight with a net bag of groceries, say, but trying to sneak a refrigerator through this minefield of debris in the pitchest of blackest darkness....

Comrades! Hai-yan's brother-in-law's foot was badly bruised when he stepped on a soccer ball (?) and crumpled beneath his corner of the refrigerator. His cries echoed throughout the building, bringing forth many an interested (but quickly frustrated) observer.

Hai-yan's sister backed into a cactus plant of prize-winning dimensions, released her grip and sent all of us stumbling back and down, fighting this huge ghost of a refrigerator in our faces, grappling literally for our lives.

We apparently also caught an edge of the refrigerator on a bicycle, and, unaware of what obstacle could be impeding us, applied extra muscle, which sent the bicycle over the railing and plummeting three stories down through the blackness, scraping and banging the whole way, to a tintinabulating finale in the concrete foyer below. The descent sounded a bit like prisoners rattling tin cups on cellblock bars. The crash itself simultaneously sent about three hundred sleeping people about one meter into the air above their beds. Now the stairwell echoed with the cries of frightened and outraged people who — our one bit of good luck — could see nothing and were too timid to investigate. We waited in the darkness, sweating, until doors closed and questions ceased, then forged ahead — to the rhythm of Hai-yan's brother-in-law's muffled *ow! ow! ow!*

We hid the refrigerator inside a stand-up closet. The next day, it was filled with chickens.

This chicken business did help to balance the FEC/US dollar and *renminbi* cash flows, comrades, but it was still not enough to compensate for the massive *renminbi* income from the watermelon sales. My only satisfaction, I thought, lay in the knowledge that the growing season could not last forever and that we would be "lucky" to get in a third gondola-load of melons before the supply was exhausted for the year.

But one evening as Chen Tai-pan, Ozaku and I were enjoying some Beijing Beer after Chen's piano practice at the Experts' Club, Ozaku mentioned how great a bargain things Chinese were to the Japanese now, given the power of the *yen.*

"Like what things?" I asked.

"Rugs," he said. "Silk rugs."

"What about silk itself?"

"Well, yes, but the quality itself is inconsistent," Ozaku said.
"What about wool rugs?" Chen asked.
"Usually they are too big," Ozaku said. "And not good in summer. But the main problem is size — made for Western consumption, and not just one or two *tatami* in size, as Japanese prefer."

Later, as I walked with Chen to the bus stop (he would never hear of taking a taxi), I asked him about the possibility of my buying rugs with *renminbi,* reselling them for *yen.*

"It's mainly a business designed to bring in foreign currency," he said. "But there may be some backlog we can tap into."

"I'd be interested especially in silk rugs, the sizes Ozaku mentioned."

"Not easy," Chen said. "But I know someone in Shanghai I can ask."

About three weeks later, comrades, I was in possession of fifty silk and fifty wool rugs, ranging from one to four *tatami* in size, and I owned them outright. Once again, our truck came in handy, and we made another midnight delivery of these rugs through the very window I am looking out now and which I stored under the two beds in here, in four stacks, as you may have guessed already from the fact that you confiscated the dozen and a half I had left — the portion, that is, which might have constituted my profit margin. Two of these, in addition, I had considered so exquisite that I just couldn't part with them. I intended these as presents for my wife and daughter. The silk one, with the sky blue border? The wool one, with that luscious deep red oval in the center? What are the chances, comrades, I could go home with at least these two?

To recapitulate: at this point, between the arrival of the second and third gondolas of watermelons, I was associated with, and in large portion responsible for these enterprises:

1. watermelon sales;
2. used bicycle sales;
3. truck rental;
4. rape and tomatoes (?) — to be confirmed by Wen;
5. cabbage and garlic;
6. Golden Chicken;
7. rug sales to Japanese tourists;
8. a potential apprentice chef training program; and
9. money-changing to the UNB and other foreign experts with white cards, an activity carried out casually in the dining hall, the true extent of which no one had an inkling.

Comrades! I believe this is a true and complete list of my economic crimes. Now you will learn how this empire unraveled.

14

COMRADES! This mood continues, feeling the lack of so many common things. Am I actually suffering that supposed disease of children, homesickness? Here is a quick catalog of what I miss today

a) My bicycle. On such a hot afternoon I would love to bicycle away to Fragrant Hills, maybe even the old Summer Palace, Empress Dowager's sweet revenge, or over-confident exploit, whatever it was. I am glad it survived the Cultural Revolution, even that grandiose and ridiculous marble boat. How could such a monstrosity remain afloat? Presumably by the Will of Heaven.

What did Mao see in this extravagant park to spare it from his overzealous minions? And why did they, who — like more young people than the world would like to admit — wanted to annihilate the oppressive past, agree to spare this historical wonder? Yes, the beauty of it is a tribute to the Chinese artisan, the craftsman, the skilled worker.

But the freedom, the freedom of bicycling, that is what I miss today. I think the narrowness of these rooms is finally stifling me. What should I be telling you now? I don't even know. Today I am confused by this mood that seems so rooted, so unshakable. I think I am even a little angry at being forever *here,* in this same place. It's unnatural for a life to be so under-stimulated, so changeless.

b) My wife. This afternoon I miss Helen more than I can say. I want to make love to her before an open window, a breeze brushing our bodies. Does this mean I am tired of China, that I feel a certain segment of my life has been played through, has reached a finale?

I could only think so because my Chinese friends have been ripped from me.

c) I miss the active life. Can't I even go for a walk, enjoy the clutch of Japanese women who come (do they still?) every day to sit by the auditorium here with their babies in strollers, their boys playing pepper as I used to, and can't I eavesdrop on their lilting, confident laughter? This business of writing, comrades, so introspective, so self-accounting, and so *public,* does not suit me. I would rather be, say, fishing, or solving some problem of computer applications. Yes, even unloading watermelons or driving the truck. I'm not afraid to work. I don't mind getting my hands dirty.

But my work has been so abstract lately, and I find it intriguing to compare this literary exercise with what I have grown accustomed to. I don't believe, and I meant to tell you this before, the logic of the printing press is any longer the logic of power. In computerdom, I feel a step closer to nature (contradictory as that may seem), to something possibly — excuse me! — holy, in that we are using the logic of the chip, yes, D-RAMS? you understand? but mainly of the crystal. And how beautiful crystals are! I like to think we are becoming the jewelers of logic.

Perhaps someday we will access the logic, the organization of, say, the very chromosome, the structure of life itself, the origins of life, to think for us. I can't conceive of anything more powerful than this, and to be in tune with the life force, I like to think, would surely mean salvation, the end to our warring, the explosion of our creativity.

But I don't know. Death is built into things, too. We must eat still, meaning we must kill something to live. Cruelty is part of the system, it seems. My worst nightmare involves these thoughts: maybe there is no purely logical space, that the other switch always opens a channel to randomness or to homogenization; or that logic itself is dream-killing, even if a kind of mental jewelry, in fact is murderous *because of* its seductive elegance.

d) I miss my daughter. Julia. Being here for eighteen months I have missed just that much of her development, of her unfolding, 1/10 of her entire life. I want to be a father again. I miss her smile, but I also miss her puzzlement and occasional outrage. Comrades, she has a powerful, primitive sense of justice that I love. I wish I could recapture it in myself. What has made me so — comparatively — cynical?

e) Jazz. This essential American music. Am I, I have sometimes asked myself, the last jazz fan? For a while, the term "jazz" was under assault, but it has survived, I think, like the music itself, so various and yet always so rooted in Africa, always with the taint of struggle against slavery, always a cry for freedom, always with room to extemporize — the antithesis of bureaucracy! — always expressing the faith in the power to extemporize our fate, and that such a fate can be beautiful after all. What a great optimism and trust is therefore the basis of jazz. Sometimes I wake up scatting, and when that happens I believe it is a day worth waking for. I feel armed.

Right now, comrades, I would like a bottle of Beijing Beer — no surprise, eh? — and to lay on my bed and listen to, say, *Song of My Father*, Horace Silver, or Duke Ellington's enormous band (and spirit), or old

Thelonious Monk, *Stuffy Turkey,* say, something weird and funny and intelligent like that.

Somewhere in China there must be a kind of Chinese "jazz", and I wonder if I would recognize it if I heard it, if anyone would. Out on some Tibetan mountainside a man is extemporizing on a reed flute, inventing the blues of his ancient culture.

f) Family. I have brothers and sisters and parents, of course. I don't think about them much, but this afternoon I do, and I discover I miss them, miss watching the Fisher/Bowdoin gene pool work out its historical and genetic destinies. How I fought to be free of them all! And I succeeded only too well.

g) My American friends, all those who forgive me my oddities, who share some of my passions. I am sure they cannot imagine my immediate predicament.

h) My Chinese friends, who, I surmise, are all in prison because of me. Who may be growing to hate me now. It's hard to bear the idea they will be reading this document. Comrades? Is that what I hear you telling me? This is a genuine form of torture: to have everything about you known to people you love.

What about Wen, for example, that bastard, what has happened to him? I don't know today whether I should call him my friend or not, a man who has snored in the bed next to mine, who has opened doors to another China I would never have known. What nerve he had! I agree with Chen that he was too ambitious and too impatient, and perhaps it is his fault, too, as well as mine, that the peculiar and wonderful human configuration we called Chen Tai-pan is now cool, comrades, coolest, is buried in the salmon-colored earth, his ashes at least, that material portion of him worth nothing, that contains not even enough phosphorus to fertilize a garden. (Think of that! And yet one microscopic sperm and egg can generate an entire being. How can we weigh this difference between life and death?)

There was this day:

Ms. Cao and I had had a particularly difficult session at work, trying to run a program we had been working on for weeks, not a particularly difficult one, but very useful, we thought, for the swine ranchers we had created it for. But it behaved quite arbitrarily and huge chunks of randomness would suddenly confront us on the screen, and we were having a hell of a time sorting it all out. All the little tricks we tried were only making things worse, and it was becoming more and more obvious we were going to have to return to square one on even this routine little assignment, a very irritating prospect indeed. We had work to do up the kazoo and never anticipated we would get hung up by a diddly assignment like this.

At the end of the day we both felt ready to kill, and felt also the need for some quietude, some tender diversion, time alone, doing something with a high probability of gratification. We would take a few hours apart to eat and wind down, and then we would meet in the evening, refreshed, with a clear motive.

"We won't even talk," Song-wen said. "I will come. We will climb in bed. Say nothing. Just be together."

"Wonderful," I said. "I hope you can stay very, very late."

"I can't promise anything," she said.

"No words," I said, "just touching, just...."

Song-wen laid a finger across my lips, smiled. Then she threw papers in a desk drawer and hurried away.

Tired as I was, I spent the early evening in sweet anticipation. We had only a few days before the third gondola of melons was to arrive and after that, time for anything but work and business would be scarce, and, if the other two nights of unloading melons were any evidence, I was going to be lame and exhausted for several days in the aftermath. I was sure Song-wen was aware of this, and we were picking our opportunity very carefully, in fact. I tried to imagine her every move, riding the bus, making dinner at home, undressing for a quick, cold shower, resting, eyes closed behind her little round glasses before she walked out to the bus again. What did she tell her husband? I wondered. Perhaps they did not even speak. That was the most comforting thought. I hated to think of him nagging her to stay home. Surely he had his suspicions by then, although quite possibly also he did not really care enough to act on them. The idea of such death of spirit saddened and irritated me. I wanted to enjoy Song-wen's presence without thinking about, worrying about the dead man she shared her apartment with. I truly hate that kind of defeat, comrades, and I am glad it is not typical. How could Song-wen cut away this weight attached to her without burdening herself in some other way?

She arrived a little earlier than I thought she would, caught me with my hair and beard still damp, and very, very relaxed. She wore only a loose cotton shift, belted at the waist, and daringly low-cut, something utterly untypical of her. As agreed, we said nothing, but she laughed silently, guiltily almost, and proffered a little bag of fruit I had never seen — something a dull yellow, the size of cherries, likewise pitted, and of a wonderful, musty sweetness. We sat on the bed and fed these to each other, placing the seeds in the ash tray which otherwise was used only to hold pocket change.

The sun was going down, but it was very warm, and the reflected glow of the sunset was too lovely to interrupt by turning on any lights. We kept our pact not to speak, and it was so pleasant to feed each other sweets and nibble fingers and necks and slowly undress each other.... Somehow our actions seemed so familiar to me, as if I were watching something that had happened once before, a long time ago, and I was seeing it again through a veil of pinkish light.

Then we were naked, comrades, and tenderly touching each other, quiet and relaxed, our fingers visiting and pleasing each other, our eagerness for each other awake but in happy abeyance. Song-wen's nipples were rigid between my lips, her sex moist, her lips warm on my face, my neck.

When the telephone rang. We both stiffened, then blushed. My telephone almost never rang, and I was in no mood for any intrusion from the real world, from Beijing or from America. We endured the seemingly endless trill, and laughed again, a slightly tense laugh, when it finally stopped. Our beautiful shell was cracked, but not broken, and we turned to each other again. Our lips brushed.

The telephone rang again.

I sore, swung off the bed, picked up the receiver.

"Yes."

"Hello, Fisher."

I recognized Wen's voice. "Yes, Wen, what is it?"

"Watermelons coming," he said.

"I know that. Wednesday."

"Yes, Wednesday."

"You didn't call to tell me that?"

"But maybe not Wednesday."

"Why not?" I sank back on the bed in despair: the world had forced its way in. Song-wen nestled against me.

"Money," Wen said.

"What do you mean, 'Money'? I gave you the money two weeks ago."

"Need more," he said.

"Bullshit," I said. "I gave you plenty of dough. What's the problem?"

"Need more," he reiterated.

"Who needs more? *You* need more, maybe, but it's not coming out of my pocket."

"Maybe no money, maybe no more melons."

"Look," I said, trying to keep my head from exploding in anger and frustration, "I gave you enough money. If those melons aren't ready, Wednesday, according to the deal we made, I am going to collect my money out of your hide."

He said something then, a series of things I couldn't understand, and I told him so. He tried again but my impatience and anger and frustration at being so interrupted stole completely my tolerance for whatever excuses he was making in whatever form of Chinglish.

"I'd better talk to him," Song-wen said, her chest against mine as she laid a hand on the telephone. "Maybe I can figure out what he's saying."

"Tell him to go to Hell in Chinese," I said, and turned over the receiver.

Song-wen talked to Wen for a while, then told me, "He says it is not the time for you to have such scruples about your loan. He is your friend, he needs money right away."

"I don't have it," I said, which was true only in a vague way — I could have come up with it if I wanted to get out of bed and set to work on it. "Besides that, you can tell him for me I'm tired of his skimming off the top to finance his little schemes. He can take the consequences like a grown-up. I'm through bailing him out."

Song-wen relayed my message, and was silent a while as Wen begged.

"He says the consequences might be very serious."

"You tell him the consequences are going to be serious if those melons aren't ready, too!"

Song-wen shook her head, but bent to the mouthpiece and told Wen what I had said. I could hear him squeaking in reply, took the receiver from Song-wen and set it in the cradle.

"It was nice," I said, "being quiet like that. God damn it!"

Song-wen flopped on her back, clearly irritated. She drew her knees up and I began to admire her trim, slender legs.

Now there was a knock on the door, and that knock sent a shiver of terror through both of us. We feared nothing more than interruption by the hotel staff, who would gossip, who could report. And with half my mind I thought Wen might have been close by and had decided to make an appeal in person, a dreadful idea with dreadful timing. Song-wen leapt into my robe and huddled at once behind the bedroom door. I drew on my trousers quickly, and a T-shirt — inside out! — and went dutifully to the door in the hall, opened it a crack.

I met the smile of Tai Hai-yan, and when I opened the door a little wider, I saw Mr. Whiz on one side of her, a young man on the other. Hai-yan, who seemed so very young at that moment, was clearly embarrassed, and very apologetic, but suggested there was something that needed to be discussed, but not in the hotel hallway.

"Oh, right," I said with a sigh. "Come on in." I drew the door to the bedroom closed as I ushered the threesome into the room where I had my desk and a few sitting chairs — what the staff would call my "office." They declined the invitation to sit, and Hai-yan introduced the young man, Wu Ko-chu, a student at Beijing University, "a new friend," she said, who was interested in talking to me about American business.

"Right now is not a good time," I said, looking at my wrist as if I had a watch on it.

"Not tonight," the young man said. "But at your convenience."

"His English so good," Hai-yan said. "Makes me mad."

I was going to ask him to call me the next day when there was another rap on the door. I excused myself and opened this time to Edith's two kids. Both were in a huff.

"A guy upstairs," the boy said, too loudly, "he ain't payin' FEC. He's got a white card, he wants to pay Chinese."

"What guy?"

"The Texan," the girl said. "The fat one."

"Did you tell him," I said, "this was not a state business, but a private enterprise?"

"We told him all that," the boy said, "but he got, like, all red in the face."

"Tell him it's O.K. tonight," I said, "but tonight only. I'll talk to him at lunch tomorrow."

"He tips for shit, too," the girl said.

"I'll take it up with him.," I said.

"He's got plenty of FEC," the boy said, apparently enjoying the complaining, or the attention, or the crisis. "Who's he tryin' to jive?"

I was just about to get the kids out of my hair when one of the hotel staff came up behind them, collared them both, occasioning a little melee, shouts, recriminations. Hai-yan, Whiz and the student joined in.

"What the hell's going on here?" I shrieked, not causing much of a diminuendo in the hub-bub.

"This guy," the boy said, "he's trying to say we can't sell chicken in here."

"He wants a bribe, that's what he wants," the girl said.

I asked Hai-yan if she could determine what the hotel attendant's beef was, a choice of words I immediately had to clarify. There followed a rapid-fire exchange, the attendant pointing to the kids, then to me.

Riding a Tiger

Whatever he said aroused Hai-yan's ire — I could see the blood rising up her neck right to her ears — so I assumed some charges had been made about her chicken business. The heads of Mr. Whiz and the students were swinging back and forth like spectators at a ping-pong match. I nodded to Edith's kids, and they got the message, drifted off into the shadows.

Where, God help me, they crashed into Krazy Kirby who had come barreling in his manic fashion into the hallway at that precise moment. He bellowed in disgust, drew in his arms and kicked out at the teens as if they were curs in the street. A scant few seconds later, Ozaku and Edith Tilden stepped out of the elevator, witnessed the assault on Edith's children, broke into cries of outrage and alarm.

"What in God's name are you doing to my children?" Edith clamored.

"Can't I walk in here without being tackled?" Kirby shot back.

Ever the mediator, Ozaku tried to get to the bottom of things. "What are you doing in this building anyway?" He spoke in a gentle, surprised tone.

"I'm a free man," Kirby said. "I want to talk to Fisher." He emphasized his remark by pointing to me.

I groaned in secret. What could he possibly want from me? As Kirby strode forward, Hai-yan was trying to explain that the attendant was sure there were rules against selling chicken in the hotel and had also made some insinuating remarks about the hygiene of her sister's operation, "which he cannot know a thing about...."

"Let's take this inside," I said, "before somebody calls a cop."

"Cop?" Hai-yan asked. "What's cop?"

"Policeman," I said. "Hello, Kirby. Come on in. Sit down. Join the party."

"What policeman?" he asked. "Why did you say that to me?"

"I'm explaining colloquial expressions to the young woman here," I said.

Kirby eyed Hai-yan and grabbed his beard in his fist. "She sure is pretty," he said.

"That's right," I said, "and she understands English. Please sit down, I'll be right with you."

"I'll just wait in there," he said, indicating the bedroom, and before I could prevent it, he had slipped inside.

I held my breath, waiting for a scream from Song-wen, but when nothing happened, I turned back to Hai-yan.

"Look," I said to her, "you tell this guy that if he wants to work for Golden Chicken, we can find something for him to do to make money. But if he tries to blackmail us I will personally pull out his tongue with a pair of pliers."

"Oh!" Hai-yan was obviously shocked. "But I don't want hire him. He's bad man."

"Make him the offer anyway."

"What is 'pliers'?"

Another knock on the door. I opened to Edith and Ozaku.

"What the hell's going on with my kids?" Edith demanded. "After all the consideration we've shown him, Kirby is out here kicking my kids!"

"A misunderstanding," I said. "Come in, will you? Actually it was the Texan giving them trouble, then this hotel jerk, trying to scare them into a little payoff."

"I know that prick," Ozaku said. "He's the one who stole my sportscoat — or tried to. I think he's on probation around here."

"Thank you!" I said. "That's just what we wanted to know."

"What means 'prick'?" Hai-yan asked.

"I'll tell you later."

"'Probation'?"

"That's more important," I said. "You tell this guy if he interferes with Golden Chicken ever again. . . ."

Now there was yet another rapping, tapping, rapping at my chamber door.

"Deng Xiao-ping," I said.

Everyone looked at me aghast.

"Who else could it be?" I asked. Opened the door, and there was Chen.

"Ah!" he said. "Good evening. I'm not interrupting anything?"

"Actually I'm not sure any more what's going on," I said.

"Oh, you have visitors."

"Join us, please. It's nothing formal."

Chen entered, and knew almost everyone present, except for the student and the hotel attendant, who were quickly introduced.

"Actually, I think I do know this young fellow," Chen said, referring to the hotel attendant, "at least I know his father." He spoke a few words of Chinese to the lad who gave a surprised "Ah!", bowed very deeply, and stood back, almost at attention. Chen then spoke to the university student.

"Yes, I speak English," Wu Ko-chu said. "And I'm studying physics."

"Of course a scientist," Chen said with a smile. "I'm sure you will contribute to China's future. Do you know Dr. Li?"

"Yes!" the student said. "I had a course from him last year."

"A very good man."

"I agree. A good teacher, too."

"So you see," Chen said, turning to me, "what a small town Beijing is, after all. We all know something about everyone. Even," he pointed to the two young men, "people we haven't met!"

Kirby, his face scarlet, stepped out of the bedroom, crossed the hall to the bathroom, and rather noisily shut the door.

"Mr. Cashman, too?" Chen asked.

"It's quite a party," I said. "What brings you here?"

"I heard Wen was trying to reach me. I thought you might know why."

"I think so," I said. "But maybe we can discuss that later."

"So mysterious!" Edith teased. "What are you up to now, Arnold, you and all your . . ." she glanced at Hai-yan, "chickens."

"Now, Edith, don't be catty, especially when folks can't fight back."

"Catty?" Hai-yan said.

"American colloquialisms are maddening," Chen said. "I heard one yesterday. Someone said, 'the situation was hairy.' 'Hairy'! Really, it makes no sense."

"Rather like this gathering," I said, "but if it does make sense, I will probably be sorry to know how. Let's start with you, Hai-yan. What was your mission?"

"This Wu Ko-chu," she said, "he wants to buy bicycle, but has not enough money."

"I'm interested," Wu Ko-chu said, "in buying on credit."

"But we don't know how," Hai-yan said, and translated for Mr. Whiz, who nodded agreement.

"It's a bad idea," I said bluntly. "As a policy. It requires too many records. Too much trouble!"

"How cruel!" Edith said. "How utterly un-American, Arnold. I'm shocked."

"Tell it to Ozaku," I said. "I think the Japanese have mastered the art of credit purchasing."

"Credit, baseball, and Beethoven," he said. "Our Western legacy!"

"And you, Edith, to what do I owe this absolutely surprising visit?"

"We wanted to warn you," Edith said, "that a certain fellow now in your bathroom was on his way, but he's a bit quicker than someone as invalided as I."

"And do you know what he wants?"

"It's a delicate matter," Ozaku said.

"In that case, Hai-yan, would you please excuse us, and bring your friend back later to discuss business? Wu, please, no hard feelings?" He gave me a wan smile, but shook my hand. "And please also, Hai-yan, tell our hotel friend here to behave himself or we'll have him fired." Niceties of good-bye followed, hand-shaking all around.

"You don't suppose he's listening, do you?" Edith nodded toward the bathroom. "Perhaps we could talk a little more privately in there?" She indicated the bedroom.

"Just step over by the window," I said.

"Prophylactics," Ozaku said.

"*What?*"

"He's in love," Edith said. "Or he thinks he's in love."

"Impossible!"

"It's true," Ozaku said. "A Canadian school-teacher."

"The ex-Mrs. Lampo," Edith said. "Isn't it delicious?"

"Mrs. Lampo," I said, "is twice his age and twice his weight. And surely sane enough to know Kirby's a bit round the bend. Sorry, Chen."

"I know that one," he said.

"Nevertheless," Edith said, "they apparently have some arrangement, or at least Kirby thinks they do, and he's absolutely certain that any Chinese prophylactics given to foreign experts have pinpricks in them."

"That's absurd!" Chen said.

"I know," Edith said, "but his mission was to sound you out, see if you had and could spare any US protection?"

"Whatever gave him the idea?" I wondered aloud.

"The same way we all get the idea," Edith said. "As Chen put it so aptly, Beijing is a small town."

"At least the You Yi Bing Guan is a small town," I said. "I'm outraged."

"Oh stow it," Edith said.

Ozaku laughed.

"Chen?" I said. "You're my witness. Are there any libel laws in China?"

"On the contrary," he said, "gossip is a common and beloved occupation."

"Why doesn't he come out of there?" Ozaku said.

"Too embarrassed," Edith said. "We'd better go. Then Kirby can make his request, and Arnold can put his shirt on straight."

"I still don't believe it," I said. "Especially not Mrs. Campo. She doesn't even *drink,* does she?"

"Opposites attract," Edith said with a philosophical shrug.

"Yes," Chen said, "but they're hard to live with!"

We laughed, and Ozaku and Edith ducked out.

"As for Wen," I said to Chen now that we were comparatively alone, "I think he needs some money. I don't know what he's into, what he's been doing with my payments, but apparently it has not all been getting to our watermelon people."

"The truck transaction was similarly tainted, wasn't it?" Chen asked.

"Can't say we weren't warned."

"He's too ambitious," Chen said. "I've tried to caution him, especially about some of the people who promise more than they can deliver."

"A damned dreamer!" I said.

"Like all of us," Chen said. "But not a realist. There must be a balance. More to the point: he's a gambler, and a bad one."

"He makes lousy bets."

"Perhaps," Chen said. "But even long shots sometimes pay off. I mean that he is a lousy gambler because money matters to him. He's therefore a scared gambler, the worst kind!"

When Chen left, I knocked on the bathroom door, then pushed it open. Kirby was just waking from a little nap in the bathtub. "Most people take off their clothes and turn on the water when they climb in there," I said.

"Not this guy," Kirby said, tapping his chest with a thumb. "I save up my thermos water. That's what I bathe in."

"You gotta be kidding."

"If it ain't boiled, it ain't touching me." Kirby climbed nimbly out of the tub and strode into the office where he stood with his hands on his hips looking out the window.

"Your girl-friend in there," he said. "She seemed pretty scared."

"I can't blame her," I said. "Strange man barging in."

"What's her name?"

"State secret," I said.

"How many you got anyway?"

"Come off it, Kirby. Do I look like Don Juan?"

"Don Quixote," he said, chuckling now. "Yeah, more like Quixote. Aren't you married?"

"Yes."

"So how do you square all that away?" he asked. "Just because she's not here, you can do what you want?"

"It's not all that simple," I said. "And none of your business."

"I want to talk about it some more," Kirby said. "Nobody talks about anything real around here. But I guess it's not the right time."

"That's true," I said. "You'll keep it under your hat, won't you?"

"Why shouldn't I?"

"I don't know. A little gossip goes a long way around here."

"Like money," Kirby said, and laughed bitterly. "Gossip info is like money around here. It stinks. Anyway, I'm going."

"Just for the record," I said, "Chinese condoms are perfectly safe. You don't need to be paranoid about them."

"Easy for you to say." Kirby blushed as deeply as I had ever seen a fellow do. He gave me a grim smile and let himself out.

When I stepped into the bedroom, Cao Song-wen was nowhere to be seen!

I called her name, and the door to the clothes cabinet swung slowly open. She was sitting there in a rather rigid posture of meditation.

"Gone at last," I said.

"Thank God!" she answered, and then we both started to laugh. She laughed so hard she almost could not extricate herself and join me on the bed where we could do nothing anyway, because every time we touched, or kissed, we broke into laughter again.

A woman's breasts — Song-wen's — trembling with laughter. Not a bad thing to remember.

Comrades!

Where was Wen?

15

Comrades, I won't go into any unnecessary detail on the unloading of gondola N° 3. With the help of Mr. Whiz's slides and the truck, the whole affair proved relatively routine.

With one significant glitch: Wen, supposed to be our truck driver, never showed up. This required us to make a hurried adjustment, and I rushed to Bu Kou Yao and drove the truck myself, finding it to my horror and anger precariously low on gasoline. This had been Wen's responsibility, and it had never occurred to me during our telephone conversation that he would be so low on both cash and scruples as to overlook this crucial detail of our operation. When I complained aloud about it, Ms. Cao noted that she had not seen him at our work unit for a couple of days and had been growing concerned about his, most unusual, absence.

"I wonder if he is hiding," she said.

"Maybe so. But from whom?"

"Whomever he owes money to."

"I don't like it," I said. "If he really is in that much trouble, he might just turn himself into a revolutionary hero and report everything to the police."

"I have trusted him so far," Song-wen said. "I still trust him. I don't believe he would betray us."

"But he could, don't you agree?"

"All living things struggle most violently just before death," she said.

"Don't talk about death!" I demanded. "Nothing we've done, nothing Wen has done deserves anyone's death."

Ms. Cao gave me a grim smile. "I hope you are right. But some debts are more serious than others."

"Oh shit," I said. "I wish I'd just given him the money."

Ms. Cao said something in Chinese.

"Which means?"

"You cannot change the course of the river."

"Of course you can," I said. "Ever hear of a dam? You people are becoming masters of flood control and. . . ."

Ms. Cao turned back to the melon pile, leaving me lecturing to myself.

Every trip I took, comrades, the gasoline gauge needle plunged deeper into the danger zone, then struck empty. I took chances, coasted every grade possible, rolled through red lights, gambling on the paucity of night-time traffic. Surely the truck was running on fumes, but it continued to run just as much as it had to and after the last load was aboard, I simply rolled the truck into a gasoline supply center and left it there, a load of melons still in it, hoping to be the first in line as soon as the facility opened. Since Wen took care of this so often, I was not even sure what papers were required or what the protocol was. I assumed he was using his taxi credentials to procure the gas, and I had nothing of that kind to unlock the gates of officialdom.

But my fears proved ungrounded and getting the gas was comparatively simple. I showed my red card and used the load of melons (leaving one, of course, for the attendants to share) to obviate my need and official status, and for the rest I think my ignorance of Chinese was my best defense. I could answer none of their questions and they shrugged and filled out the forms. I paid in cash. All was well. It was a beautiful, dry morning, already hot, comrades, and I confess I like driving a truck — especially a huge and old one which makes no pretense at maintaining speed, which everyone excuses for its lumbering ways. I felt like a spy, like an alien from another planet come to secretly observe a square of life on earth. Although I had a meeting scheduled early at the work unit office, I did not hurry. I met Chen at the unloading site and we took our sweet time swinging the melons down.

He handled the melons so gently, his pianists hands large and knobby, and I think now they must also have been the hands of a lover. He worked with a graceful rhythm, and the only sign that the labor was fatiguing him as it would any other mere mortal was a dark line of sweat which appeared in the crown of his blue Mao cap. He did not talk much, but what he did say showed me a man who had been through every kind of nastiness and yet had emerged without any trace of bitterness or cynicism — a human miracle.

This was the last I would see of him alive.

16

N*ow you will tell us the circumstances of Chen's death, how you came to learn of it, what you found.*
Comrades, this is the hardest part!
It is crucial.
I know this. I want to get everything exactly right, but I have thought about this so much, dreamed about it so much, that I am not sure what I truly remember and what I have imagined. Sometimes I think I will see him, you know, again. A knock on the door and ah! there he is. It was all a bad dream after all.
Do you feel the shock of his death has affected your judgement or your sanity?
Everything about China has affected my judgement and sanity, comrades! Who am I? What am I doing here? Much more of this and I will turn into another Krazy Kirby. To me, Chen was a very special human being. To find him. . . .
How did you first learn of his death?
I was in my office, about four hours after I had left Chen at the Beijing Hotel and parked the truck in Bu Kou Yao.
When I parked, by the way, I saw Dong Xidi and I asked her if she had seen Wen, but I don't think she understood my question very well, and I didn't understand her reply. I thought she said that, yes, she had seen him on Monday (the night he had called while Ms. Cao was with me) and that he was driving a load of watermelons somewhere. This made no sense to me and I assumed she was confused about his reason for taking the truck, didn't know it, really, perhaps had been lied to, and only knew Wen was a key man on our watermelon team. So Wen perhaps had used the truck that night, or rented it to someone and was delivering it — I don't know. And I don't believe Dong Xidi will know, either, though I'm sure you have questioned her already.
So I went to my office and endured this awful meeting. Both Ms. Cao and I were fighting to stay awake, and I was having one of those particularly awful periods when you are so tired you are dreaming while awake, mixing up your dreams with what is happening before your eyes. Three or four cups of tea was not helping in the least, just making me all the more uncomfortable. So I was falling asleep and crossing my legs to keep from wetting my pants and somehow pay attention to the meeting

and also shake off this creeping dread about Wen and his problems. The meeting droned on into the lunch hours, but civilization finally prevailed and we were released. I sped to the toilet, rather unceremoniously shouldering past several others on their way as well, and the relief was quite overwhelming.

I returned to the office to meet with Song-wen, and as I approached she pulled me inside and slammed the door. Her face was ashen, and she gagged as if she were about to be sick.

She managed: "I think Wen has been found. Dong Xidi just called. We must go at once. He's there. He's dead."

"Bu Kou Yao? *Dead?*"

"It was a very confused message. I think that's what she said."

"Oh my God."

"What are we going to do?"

"First," I said, "verify." And then I asked if the police had been notified.

"Not directly. Not by Dong Xidi. We must hurry."

Once again, China proved immune to the immediacy of our needs. Unable to flag a taxi, we had to walk several blocks to the nearest hotel, there to be told there was a substantial line of tourists waiting for service ahead of us, and very few cars available.

We resorted to the next most ultimate crime in Beijing, comrades, found in the tangle of bicycles parked around the corner one that was unlocked, and stole it. Song-wen rode (another crime) on the cross bar between my arms as I humped through the summer afternoon and arrived in Bu Kou Yao bathed in sweat.

Dong Xidi trundled out of her brick cottage, grabbed me by the arm, and towed me through a narrow lane to what once must have been an interior garden, a courtyard, but was now a communal playground and meeting place.

Our truck was there, comrades, its tailgate down, the bed was empty, but immediately beneath the truck was a huge pile of watermelons, at one extreme of which was a blanket with a bulge in the center of it. By words and gestures, Dong Xidi led us to understand we should look under the blanket.

Sick, and sad, I lifted the corner of the blanket, and I saw at once a pair of feet and legs that disappeared under the pile of melons. I dropped the blanket and steeled myself, then threw it aside and plunged into the melon pile.

"Wen, you poor bastard," I muttered, "forgive me. . . ."

Riding a Tiger

And then I saw it was not Wen, comrades, but Chen! I felt as if I had been hit a staggering blow, and I turned and collapsed in Ms. Cao's arms, who had all she could do to hold me upright. Dong Xidi braved a look, too, and when she saw her old comrade — badly battered about the face, bleeding from the mouth — she exploded into a terrible shrieking.

"Not Wen," I said to Song-wen.

"Thank God," she said. "Who?"

"Chen."

Now we both fell to the ground. Dong Xidi fell on top of us. We were a confused, writhing mass, of absolutely no comfort to each other. I had no idea what to do, but it was perfectly clear that my life in China was over. Some terrible line had been crossed, and now the shock wave and the repercussions would follow.

Chen, slapped down!

"What will we do now?" Song-wen sobbed.

There was no answer to her question.

17

SHORTLY AFTERWARDS *you were arrested in the company of Dong Xidi, a.k.a. Bu Kou Yao Ma, and Cao Song-wen.*

Yes. We were on our way to a telephone to notify the police of Chen's death. However, it must be said in all truth, that we did not intend to return to the courtyard, but merely to report the death. We were in shock, not thinking clearly.

The arrest came as a great relief to me, but after some confused conversation with the young patrolman — unarmed, by the way — Ms. Cao realized we were being taken into custody for stealing a bicycle! Therefore, Dong Xidi was allowed to slip away and make the telephone call that brought the officers into Bu Kou Yao and into the knowledge of Chen's "accident".

Meanwhile, the young patrolman took down our names and examined our red cards and was determined to report our behavior to our work unit. Somehow we managed to turn the bicycle over to him and express our great sorrow for the rashness of our action, and claimed several dire emergencies at once. Cao Song-wen was very cool and official and persuasive to this young fellow, comrades, and once again we found ourselves "free".

We bussed to my hotel, shivering with dread, unable to decide what course of action we should take, whether we should come forward with the truth — and cause difficulty to so many people — or simply hope that Chen's death would not be linked to our watermelon enterprise and the people in it. I, of course, being a foreigner, was not immune from the laws of China, but perhaps had the greater protection of my government behind me. So although I might have liked to come forward at once, I had my colleagues and friends to consider.

By the time we reached the hotel, we realized that we had erred greatly in running off from Bu Kou Yao, that we must have Chen's murder/accident/death looked into in the fullest possible way.

This resolution we could not implement, because as soon as we walked onto the hotel grounds, I was arrested again — this time by two officers with guns strapped on, and big fellows, quite experienced and no-nonsense fellows, who took me one under each arm and lifted me off my feet and propelled me into the sidecar of a motorcycle.

Riding a Tiger

Song-wen, white with fear and yet still mercilessly official and pragmatic, discovered that this time I was being arrested for corrupting the morals of a Chinese citizen and entering into unauthorized business contracts. I had no idea whom or what businesses were being referred to. But Song-wen found herself being lectured to in the name of Tai Hai-yan, being told, in effect, that she was a strumpet tool of capitalist corrupters. This complaint, she sorted out, had been brought forward by Wu Ko-chu.

"Who?" I said, dizzy, disoriented.

"I don't know!"

"Oh, Christ! It's that kid who wanted to buy a bicycle on credit! He's nuts about Tai Hai-yan, too. He thinks I've seduced her."

Song-wen staggered a little, but held on. "Two arrests," she said. "One trivial, one bad."

"Maybe one to come," I said.

The motorcycle ripped into life and Song-wen's advice was drowned out. The second officer, still preaching, climbed in beside me! And sat there on the rim of the sidecar, his feet and legs jammed along my back. We crackled away, and that, comrades, was also my last glimpse of Song-wen, her face contorted in agony, running after me, halting, running again, then stumbling off in helpless misery.

I don't know how they do it, comrades, but the policeman who arrested me, in full bore through the streets of Beijing, lit up cigarettes and smoked them! The ashes kept slashing into my eyes.

18

When the police arrived at Bu Kou Yao, there was no truck. Only the melons and Chen's corpse. How do you explain this?
I can't.
A few hours later we arrested Mr. Wen in the truck you say was at Bu Kou Yao. He had been speeding and crashed into a utility pole. He said he had been using the truck all week to haul furniture and make extra money. Do you deny this?
The truck, our truck, was in Bu Kou Yao when we arrived.
Why don't you tell us frankly what was in the watermelons?
What do you mean? Surely you don't mean.... Listen! I got those melons off the gondolas and we sold them in the streets in good faith to good citizens! There was nothing in those watermelons but watermelon!
Did Wen always drive the truck after it had been loaded?
Mostly Wen. Sometimes Chen. I told you, the last time, I drove.
Were you not told to look for specially marked melons?
Marked?
You can read Chinese, can you not?
Only a little. A few hundred characters.
Do you recognize this mark?
No.
Look closely.
"Bao yu," maybe. Does it mean something like "precious jade"?
You have never seen this mark before?
Not on any melons. Not that I recall. Unless....
Yes?
I thought it was a brand name. The name of a commune or something.
So you saw this mark on some of the melons.
I'm afraid so.
On several or a few?
Very few. Very rare. I almost forgot it.
But you unloaded at night always.
Yes.
And it's possible that melons were marked but you didn't see them.
Of course. But wait a minute....
That is all for today, Mr. Fisher.
Wait a minute....

19

COMRADES, I WANT VERIFICATION.
About what?
Yesterday I received a message.
How did you receive a message?
I have friends. I have a telephone.
No one telephoned you.
Ah?
No one visited you.
That's where you're wrong. Someone called up to me from the street.
What did he say?
He or she. I'm not telling which. They said: "Your Chink girlfriend is dead. Suicide."
Who was the message referring to?
You tell me. Ms. Cao, or more likely, Tai Hai-yan.
Neither of these women is dead.
Don't lie to me!
Don't shout at us. We do not lie to you.
Is one in critical condition, then?
We do not have to discuss the welfare of other principals in this case.
Tell me, goddammit! How can I do anything until I know? I'm worried sick.
We will need to make sure you receive no more messages.
My friends will find a way. Some things you cannot keep secret! You cannot kill someone and hide that fact. China, surely, is not becoming the Argentina of the generals, disappearing people?
Of course not. We are not savages.
1967 to 1976.
The Cultural Revolution is over.
Is it?
Mr. Fisher, Tai Hai-yan is in the hospital after attempting suicide.
Ah?
She will recover. She was not aware that Ms. Cao had become your mistress.
You told her this.
She was not aware of how you were exploiting her. It was necessary to destroy certain illusions.

How did she do this thing?
She sat in the bathtub. She cut her wrists.
With *what,* for Christ's sake?
A broken tea cup.
Ai. . . . Ai, ai, ai.

20

No report today.

21

22

Mr. Fisher, you must finish. You are very close to finishing. We have waited three days.

23

Maybe you should know something about my life in America, what it was like before I came here. My work. My wife. My daughter. Krazy Kirby, I told you, asked the essential question: "Why did you come?" I did not think that I came to kill people, or destroy them.

I want to start everything over now, because everything has changed. I want to go back to the beginning and start over.

Chen.

Hai-yan.

But what else will happen if I do? What curse have I laid on all the rest of the people I met here? What curse was laid on me?

When I look out the window and see someone ride by on a bicycle, I collapse. She was so beautiful on a bicycle.

But nothing *accounts*. . . .

24

YOU DON'T WANT TO KNOW my dreams. But here's one: I'm driving a car — something I haven't done since I've been here — and I feel confident I am driving very well. I'm driving along a road which is only wide enough for the car, and the road winds through the mountains and is very curvy (you can never see too far ahead) and it drops off precipitously on the passenger side. The very edge of my outside wheels is on the very edge of the dropoff, but I am driving so well that these two edges are in constant contact.

My passenger, however, an attractive woman of my age, is quite nervous about the speed we're traveling and the hazardousness of the road.

Her agitation causes a shadow of a doubt to flicker across my own mind, the merest shadow, and in the dream this doubt, or reflection, is a palpable, white wave that I can see and feel moving across my brain which, in the dream, is momentarily visible, as in some kind of X-ray.

As we continue our ascent, clouds crumple against the mountainside and over the road, making driving even more precarious.

Then I realize, comrades, I am not really in control at all, that the tension I feel in the wheel, that pressure I feel of the turning car, the torque of the wheels on the road, is all an illusion which persuades me I am in control: something else, or the car itself has command and is even more unerring and capable and kind to my own interests and that of my passenger than I could ever be.

To confirm this, I only need to let go of the wheel. I am certain that I can do this without accident, but I also know that if I do, my pleasant, attractive companion will become terrified.

Therefore, I do not let go.

25

How far back must I go, comrades? What was the original sin? Our histories — how do they shape us and the contours of our experience? I'm speaking of our times, the evolving of our national luck, or destiny, which we begin to see is international, and global. What a tiny little planet after all!

I was four years old when the Atomic Bomb, "Fat Boy", as they called it, was dropped on Japan. I do not remember that. What I remember from that year is my father killing a goose I considered a pet — the head coming off cleanly, and then the white feathers turning scarlet, a purple fountain pulsing from the open neck.

When you execute a man or a woman, comrades, with a shot to the base of the skull, how does the body behave? How does the man feel who pulls the trigger? And surely things go wrong! I have seen animals butchered (I am talking now of the Korean War years, when you and I were not yet teens) and I know things can go wrong. I have seen a pig with an eye shot out crashing around a barn, have seen chickens with their throats slit flutter upside down over barrels, a foot, or both feet coming free from their twine nooses....

I'm thinking of Hai-yan, comrades, the blood unscrolling in the warm water.

And of Chen, bleeding from the mouth. How hard must a man be hit to stun him to death? Did the tailgate fall, or was he held there and the tailgate brought down with deliberate violence? Why was he there? Had he gone to intercede with, to plead for Wen?

Tell me, comrades!

I am not blameless.

26

Comrades!

Today I am thinking that it would be in the interest of the Party and of harmony for all concerned if I took it upon myself to compose for you something besides a new version of my self-criticism. One reason for this is I have traced the roots of my difficulties back to the Big Bang, and this is a mental journey too complex and tedious for anyone's edification, let alone pleasure. Instead, with your permission, I would like to persuade you of my rehabilitation by offering to create for your use Chen Tai-pan's diary. We all know that the creation of diaries for "evidence" is a standard intelligence procedure world-wide. In the US we have four notable products — possibly! for who can dare to dispute their authenticity? — including the diaries of Arthur Bremer, Lee Harvey Oswald, Sirhan Sirhan, and James Earl Ray. No one seems surprised that these assassins all indulge in the nineteenth century practice of recording their daily thoughts and the important events in their lives. Allow me to perform this service for you, and my late friend.

This would be easier, obviously, if I had my computer. What I intend to do, comrades, is to create two or three alternate versions of each statement, each event, from which you can choose any or all that suit your version of Chen Tai-pan's psychological profile and the message, or Truth, you wish to communicate by promulgating "his version" of events. I trust you will not find this utter sacrilege.

As I say, if I had my computer, you could make your selection simply by pressing F1, F2, F3, or ALT keys. And so:

Scenario A:

F1: Tonight went to You Yi Bing Guan with Ozaku my Jap. lang. teacher, a kind, witty fellow. Met several foreign experts, including one Arnold Fisher, whose beady eye and sneering lip and look of cold command marked him as a potentially dangerous perpetrator of decadent ideas. Therefore, determined to befriend him in order to spy on his activities. His obvious weaknesses are women and Beijing Beer. Claims computer expertise.

F2: Friend Ozaku introduced me tonight to several foreign experts, including one American a Mr. Fisher, a middle-aged, balding, somewhat silly computer programmer with a taste for beer and an eye for the ladies. His ignorance about China is so profound as to constitute a danger to himself, and I think I had better keep an eye on him to make sure he doesn't get into trouble.

    F3: At Ozaku's tonight. Met foreign experts, including one dumpy little computer programmer with unpronounceable name. I'm sure I can manipulate him to line my own pockets. He's quite stupid, but imagines himself smart — easy pickings!

    ALT: After a dinner with Ozaku at the You Yi Bing Guan:
Among the volleyball nets and stanchions
tonight:
the international smile of piano keys!

Scenario B:

    F1: Continued my subtle positioning and investigation of the capitalist Fisher tonight by playing some sentimental Western classics on the piano and continuing to lose a few *kuai* at gin rummy — not easy to do, given the man's stupidity. He sounded me out on prospects for selling watermelons at key city locations and I expressed interest, hoping to get a more in-depth picture of the extent of his nefarious operations and the other criminals involved. Surely watermelons are just a front.

    F2: Had a fine time practicing piano tonight and playing an American gambling game called "gin rummy", though I lost a few *kuai*. Will teach them all mahjong some night and get it back. The programmer Fisher proves an entertaining companion, but it seems he has also got himself involved in a watermelon selling operation and needs help finding sales locations. I supposed that if I don't do something to help him, he'd only run into serious problems. So I tried to think of some places where he could sell melons and stay out of trouble....

    F3: So Fisher is in watermelons! He's got a line to Xinjiang melons, he thinks, and needs a place to sell them. The idiot! It's perfect for us. We'll let him and his stupid friends haul the melons for us, and take the rap for whatever comes down. Meanwhile, it's all as if I'm doing *him* a favor. Let him think he's selling melons! Must make a call to Zuotian....

    ALT: After Chopin and Gin Rummy at the Experts' Club:
Rain on the dark, green tiles
a xylophone; in western China
the rain drums bass notes
on our sweetest fruit!

Scenario C:

Mr. Fisher, we are not interested in this game. You are wasting our time. Please finish your self-criticism. You need only to say a few words more. We warn you this is the last opportunity.

But comrades! You said this endeavor was for my own good! I thought being in business here was also for my own good, that it would bring me love, and adventure, and money. Which it did. But the wholesale price, comrades! The price!

Perhaps I need to do this to find my own perspectives, to find *reasons,* some *reality*. . . .

Any so-called diary of Chen's will not be part of the official record.

But, comrades, I was only trying to help!

Terminus of official record. See Appendices A, B, and C, however.

Appendix A

OCT. 3, 1988: Comrade Sun reported to us this morning in the presence of a man unknown to us who, laughing and nodding, claimed to be Arnold Fisher, and who was found in Fisher's room, drinking Fisher's tea and eating Fisher's breakfast bread. He has not swerved from this falsehood since questioning began. Mr. Fisher, in the meantime, has not been located.

A quick investigation has led us to identify the man in our custody as Kirby Cashman, under contract to Beijing Canneries here. A check of flight records to Tokyo this morning confirms that a "Kirby Cashman", with all appropriate documents, including exit visa, left Beijing for that City at 5 AM. For reasons we have yet to clarify, Mr. Cashman apparently traded documents with Mr. Fisher, and attempted also to trade identities with him.

We are in communication at this moment with the Canadian Embassy in hopes of providing true documentation for Mr. Cashman in order to expedite his departure; and with the American Embassy to protest Mr. Fisher's escape from justice. There is little hope, we feel, of our request for extradition being honored.

Mr. Cashman, to an even greater extent than Mr. Fisher, has proven an unruly and uncooperative detainee. He also will not drink Wu Sying Beer and is scraping the food we give him into the toilet or out the window. And he still insists he is Arnold Fisher.

Appendix B

Nov. 3, 1988: Today Mr. Arnold Fisher was declared *persona non grata* henceforth in China, and this communiqué has been passed on to our consulates in America and Canada along with expressions of concern over the refusal of the USA to extradite him for trial here. The American Embassy has proffered the absurd explanation that authorities in the US State Department do not believe he will receive a fair trial.

The self-criticisms of other principals in this investigation have revealed a high level of rehabilitation. Cao Song-wen and Tai Hai-yan have acknowledged being exploited by Mr. Fisher for his personal gain and gratification. The committee has recommended a year of rustication for both. Ms. Cao's service will begin at once, at a watermelon commune in Xinjiang. Ms. Tai's will begin as soon as her health is restored. Dz Jr-shi ("Mr. Whiz" in this document) has been made aware not only of his own exploitation but of how he contributed to a false economy and the exploitation of his working comrades. He has been fined and returned to his work unit. The unowned bicycles at the You Yi Bing Guan have been impounded.

Wen Da-xing awaits further inquiry. His explanation of his association with Mr. Fisher is unconvincing and contains notable contradictions. We are, therefore, extending the investigation to include many of his relatives.

Dong Xidi (a.k.a. Bu Kou Yao Ma) has been assigned to sweeping the streets in her neighborhood as an example of trying to take advantage of new freedoms.

Kirby Cashman was yesterday released into the custody of the Canadian Embassy.

Appendix C

Dec. 27, 1988: The following letter was sent to us folded inside a Western "Christmas card". On the front of the card is a picture of "Santa Claus" in a sleigh next to bag filled with toys. He is racing down a snowy slope, smiling and waving. The legend inside the card reads: "Happy Holidays to One and All", and the card is signed "Arnold Fisher family". The letter itself is written on You Yi Bing Guan airmail stationery and is signed "A. Fisher" also. We include it for the sake of thoroughness and for possible future reference.

Merry Christmas, comrades!

Tonight I am sitting alone in my home in America, a humble house, cheaply furnished, but very comfortable by common standards elsewhere in the world. I feel I must confess that although I was desperate to leave China, I am suffering something like "culture shock" right now back here in the evangelical scientific Twentieth Century. I think the degree of my desperation and my fear that I had wallowed into something over my head ought to be proved by the expedient I took to flee. Of course it was Kirby who communicated the news of Hai-yan's "death", and in fact he had been in my very room to deliver this awful, and fortunately erroneous datum. You posted a guard on the lawn before my balcony, but Kirby did not approach me from below — but from above, mad *deus ex machina*. He started in the room of a Texas friend, a UNB member in good standing, and lowered himself balcony by balcony using scaffolding that had been erected for repointing the masonry, and then "borrowed" a plank to traverse the last level. Yes, Kirby wore a hard-hat and carried a clipboard and I think that, if anything, the sight of such a handsome, purposeful, Western fellow descending the bulwarks and crossing their balconies probably gave the tourists a sense that all was in good hands. He would smile gravely and nod a greeting, and as long as he didn't talk to anybody, how were they to know a rather deranged and somewhat dangerous person was just beyond the window-pane?

In any case, he arrived, merry and cheerful, and feeling a bit in my debt, I think, because I did, after all, bequeath him my prophylactic supply, and considering it a great *coup* to turn over to me his passport, his credit cards, his exit visa, his red and blue cards, and his plane tickets! Comrades, I was aghast at this ploy, and at Kirby's delight in offering me the freedom that he so desperately longed for and so plainly needed.

When I at first refused, he said, "Hey! You want to die?"

"No," I said.

"If it was drugs in those melons," he said, "you're dead."

"Wen wouldn't have taken the chance," I said. "He wouldn't have endangered us all like that?"

"Wanta bet?" Kirby said. "More precisely: are you willing to bet your life?"

I traded credentials. I climbed the scaffolding to the Texan's room. And taxied away.

So I don't know yet, comrades, what was in the melons that concerned you — dope, or computer chips, or nylon stockings or atomic secrets, whatever the world trades in these days. I prefer to think there was nothing in them but what was supposed to be there: that good, juicy melon.

Oh well. My China days are done. I leave a dead man and embittered former friends and lovers behind — a disgusting legacy, even if not the worst I ever heard about. I can't collect on this disaster. It's my legacy, and you can add to my confession that it pains me deeply. It pains me deeply that I cannot return to friends and enthusiastic colleagues, too, and if I can do anything to remove the stigma of my tenure there . . . but that's not realistic. I'm dreaming again, comrades, and as for dreams I know already, you don't want to hear them.

I see in the paper tonight that the students at Beijing University are demonstrating again — not rioting, as in Korea, or protesting, as in Japan, or hurling rocks, as in the Gaza Strip, or firing bullets as in Northern Ireland, but politely demonstrating. After all, only a fool would kick a tiger. And their requests — not demands — comrades, to those of us in the West, seem so reasonable and very tame, really, it is hard to imagine the state being aroused. Perhaps you feel, as I do, that any effort exerted to expand one's limits — to be freer — is just a down payment on a long mortgage. The first pennies paid, you will have the house, or die trying.

What is the price of freedom? I ask. Is it the time you spend fighting for it, the scars of battle? Nobody, I notice, hands it to you. Not your parents, not your teachers, not your church, not any institution which might be expected to celebrate and promote the existence of another. Sometimes even people whom you love cannot give you freedom (and vice versa!) and these are the hardest, most painful battles of all. We want the others to be created in our image and an odd hairstyle can make a whole culture wince. Comrades, I was the first person on my block (since

Riding a Tiger

maybe the 1890s) to wear a beard, and I have an antique aunt who still demands I "shave that damned thing off!" My daughter, at least, has not yet resorted to pink hair. Even rebellion, it seems, is done in packs and has its rules. We want agreement, "harmony", as you say, not eccentricity.

I suppose the price of freedom is also time: the time it takes to learn anything. To learn to live is a never-ending process, which makes the price of freedom, alas, infinite, and perfect freedom itself unattainable. So we are free by degrees and dignified by the degree of our freedom. I mean it, comrades. I say the same things to Americans, who believe themselves free and are too often smug in this belief.

I've just described something that is a meritocracy of a kind, which values the struggle to be free. And there I was, kissing your butts, begging for more beer. What respect could I have earned by that? By my own standards I was an abject failure, who did not struggle — has not struggled — very much. My income now, if translated into the budget of a nation, would denote a civilization more devoted to the production of ale and books, computer accessories, watermelons and love than anything else. What US politician could say the same and declare: "I stand on my record", and then expect a single vote?

Inevitably I seem to get caught between my own ideals and an awful moral inertia. I pay my taxes, even the portion which builds the thermonuclear arsenal which, like Krazy Kirby, I am sometimes certain — nauseatingly so — will unhinge all thinking life, leaving this bright blue planet to a few insect automatons. Why doesn't that thought frighten us enough, shame us enough to dare to be different, to double up the fist and say, "I want to be free of this terror?" What chains bind us when even the ultimate horror is at stake? Isn't even the reality of our conditions a goad to free action? What primitive man or woman seeing a tiger in the mouth of the cave would not pick up a spear or a rock?

Surely once those Beijing University students learn to demonstrate, the activity will become a rite of growth. All roads to perfection are infinitely long. China is not perfect. America is not perfect. We would be insane to expect perfection, and in fact the best that sometimes can be hoped for is the avoidance of disaster. Krazy Kirby used to reason — erroneously, I think — that if the Big One didn't land right now, then we had twenty minutes to breathe easy. He was often checking his watch. People rarely protest starvation because they are too weak to do so. I'm sure some tyrant has made a note of this. I know Krazy Kirby used to discourse on the possibility of protein wars, when, you know, the planet reaches that stage of overpopulation when most available protein exists only in the form of other human beings. If imagining perfection is madness, is it equally insane to imagine such a Hell?

Comrades!

What do we need?

Rest easy: I am not going to supply a manifesto, since the world has plenty enough of those. I won't pretend to speak for anyone else. But I know what I want, and I have China and some Chinese people, in part, to thank for that. Yes, I owe you something after all!

What I want is the slightest excuse, the slightest opportunity to be real. With Tai Hai-yan I found it in ways I had forgotten, ways that had been closed off to me. Even animals play! Isn't it a shame that human beings cannot purr?

With Cao Song-wen I found myself a teacher and a goad, and yet also an ardent admirer, a wonderful paradox of instruction and worship of a woman at least my equal. I felt it a great privilege to enter her world when she opened the door. She feels now, I suppose, that I violated the premises, but that was never my intent, never the spirit of my privileged exploration! Oh, to walk again so freely in the palace of another!

And Chen? He showed me what a man can be. Yes, I have my American heroes and heroines, but Chen added a dimension that even this Pantheon lacks: a sense of at-homeness in the world, of personal accomplishment and a detachment from the klutziness of everyday life that is part of the grit and stumble of humanity. He was a man with high ideals who did not expect too much. I'm jealous of him, too: to learn with his ease! To love with his gracefulness!

Wen I know from other worlds. He is a too familiar type, perhaps because I see myself in him: a little like the big-footed clown who in reaching for his hat kicks it still farther out of reach. Yes, he is all too much like me! It would be fine to exorcise this part of me, this impatient, over-eager, grasping part of me. At the same time, I know all too well now — Chen, forgive me! — this is a short existence. If I grow old, if I survive, what will I have to remember that will make me feel I have lived a *life,* and not a charade? I do not scorn Wen, for all the trouble he made. I aided and abetted him. I am his brother. We ride into town. We rob banks.

At home now, comrades, though I have seen these other potentials in myself, and have become an outcast who cannot bear to set foot in the patent obscenity of the shopping mall, I am sinking into old habits, comfortable, trouble-free ways of being. I love my wife and daughter, and admire them, and I want them to succeed in their lives, on their terms. Suppose my wife said, "I am taking a job in France next year." Would I feel terrified and abandoned? Betrayed? Or would I say, "Good! That's something I think you should do"? Comrades! I would do all of these things, and all at once. Why not? It's the computer age! Do we have to be chained by our own fears, or, even worse, the fears of others? Do we rope others down because we are afraid for them? Listen closely and you will hear the knocking of knees from around the world. What a rattling of bones drives this planet! Are we even afraid to be alone?

So I am through confessing, comrades. Tomorrow I will get in my car and I will drive along the polluted river to the obscene shopping mall, and contain my disgust enough to carry out our Christmas rituals. Nothing I buy will ever express the love I have for Helen and Julia, the rest of my family, my friends. But I don't know what else to do. I have not yet discovered my path to freedom in this sphere. Santa Claus still has me by the balls. It's a rather common, slightly desperate and unfulfilling act, this buying of holiday gifts. What *thing* can I give them that will help them to be free?

Ah! I have it.

Bicycles!

Happy New Year, and Farewell.

About the author

Robert Abel is an American writer, who has written two previous novels, *Freedom Dues,* a comic historical novel, *The Progress of a Fire,* about the Vietnam generation, and three collections of stories: *Ghost Traps* (the title story of which won the 1989 Flannery O'Connor Short Fiction Award), *Full-Tilt Boogie* and *Skin and Bones.*

He is a graduate of the University of Massachusetts Writing Program and was awarded a National Endowment for the Arts Creative Writing Fellowship in 1978. He was born and raised in the Midwest, where he spent several years as a college instructor, editor and journalist. He now lives and writes full-time in North Central Massachusetts.

Robert Abel worked in Beijing as a foreign expert in 1987, and taught English through literature at the Beijing Foreign Studies University in 1994. On his return to Beijing in 1997 (teaching English again) he says he found *Riding a Tiger* seeming more prophetic than fantastic.

Cheung Chau Dog Fanciers' Society
by Alan B Pierce

"A rare read indeed. Not only is it an accurate slice of Hong Kong life — touching on heroin smuggling, money laundering, corruption in the police force as well as in one of Hong Kong's most wealthy and powerful Chinese families — but it also depicts a very local journey of self-discovery. A superb description of insular life, complete with beery expatriates, ploddish village policemen, arm-wrestling triads and masses of day-trippers.
　　A thriller with a difference." — **Richard Cook**, *Hongkong Standard*
"One of the best Hong Kong novels ever written. It puts James Clavell to shame." — **Rupert Winchester**, *HK Magazine, Metro Radio*
　　"There are too few good novels set in Hong Kong's modern era. This is one of the better ones, with Pierce at his best when writing from the heart about the texture of life in a special place."
— **Katherine Forestier**, *South China Morning Post*

ISBN 962-7160-38-5

Temutma
by Rebecca Bradley and John Stewart Sloan

Temutma, a *kuang-shi*, a monster similar to the vampire of European legend, is imprisoned beneath Kowloon Walled City in Hong Kong by his ancient keeper Wong San-bor. The monster escapes when the Walled City is being cleared for demolition. Hungering for blood it begins a horrifying series of murders, starting with the Ralston family on the Peak, saving only the daughter Julia for later enjoyment. A policeman, Scott, questions her, and as the deaths continue night after night comes to realise what he is pursuing — and is then pursuing him and Julia.

ISBN 962-7160-47-4

Hong Kong Rose
by Xu Xi

Hong Kong Rose is the novel which marks the end of British Hong Kong and the ascendancy of Hong Kong writers as a voice of their own on the world English language literary scene. Hong Kong's story has never been told so true.

From a crumbling perch with a view of the Statue of Liberty, Rose Kho, Hong Kong girl who made it, lost it, and may be about to make it or lose it again, reflects, scotch in hand, on a life that "like an Indonesian mosquito disrupting my Chinese sleep" has controls of its own. Or, like a wounded fighter plane of the type her father used to fly, no controls at all. Xu Xi, the gifted, uncompromising storyteller, gives us a Hong Kong that sheds its artifice as a snake sheds its skin, only to grow new artifice. In Hong Kong Rose, petals metamorphose into scales that shine like mirror glass windows, reflecting equally the courage, cowardice and compromise of one of the world's great cities.

ISBN 962-7160-55-5

Daughters of Hui
by Xu Xi

Xu Xi's characters are the antithesis of the exotic Asian heroines of so much Western fiction. They roam the earth in search of an answer to Lao Tzu's ancient question, "Your name or your person, Which is dearer?" They drive tollways and pick up strangers. They fight the ghosts of a hundred generations with divorce lawyers. And even in their suicides they are self-possessed.

"Xu Xi is a Hong Kong writer who does not write like the typical 'Hong Kong writer' and speaks with more authority because of it."
— **Todd Crowell**, *Asiaweek*

ISBN 962-7160-40-7

Getting to Lamma
by Jan Alexander

The subject of Jan Alexander's first novel is a young American woman who carves out a place for herself in Hong Kong. To do so she must deal with an old flame, a handsome young Shanghainese, two babies and an elderly Chinese nurse. This is Hong Kong expatriate society at the countdown to Chinese takeover, with the harsh realities of China no longer kept at bay. There is also a deeper story, of growing into a life, an imperfect but satisfactory life that finds its purpose on Lamma, an unfashionable offshore island far removed from the expectations and ambitions of a once fashionable New Yorker.

ISBN 962-7160-49-0

Walking to the Mountain
by Wendy Teasdill

This is the story of a journey made on foot across Tibet to Mount Kailash. Kailash has been attracting pilgrims of all religions for thousands of years, but until recently only a handful of Westerners had ever been there.

Wendy Teasdill hitch-hiked from Lhasa and walked the last four hundred miles alone, between the Himalaya and the Trans Himalaya, living on hard-tack biscuits, noodles and nettles. She survived, to tell the tale of the people, landscapes, dangers, delights and thoughts that she encountered on the way.

"Wendy Teasdill provides a vivid personal account of how she was drawn to Mount Kailash. Inspired by the beauty of the landscape and her admiration for the Tibetan people she met, she reached her goal."
— **The Dalai Lama**

"A testament to courage and commitment. Its style is crisp, poignant and quietly stirring. The narrative has the steady pounding beat of the lone trekker with a mission." — **Vernon Ram**, *Asiaweek*

ISBN 962-7160-27-x

Woman to Woman
poems by Agnes Lam

Agnes Lam belongs to a generation in both Hong Kong and Singapore for whom life has become cautiously cerebral. Indeed, "My cerebral child" is the title of her best known poem, in which she asks *Child of my imagination / what do you know / of the wombless world?* The answer is a silence, to which the new-found wealth and refinement of Hong Kong and Singapore cannot minister. Even when writing about death, her language floats above her emotions, mindful, for example, about the affluence that embalms preparations for her mother's funeral: *Silk underwear, embroidered shoes, / our last chance to spend on you. / Your favourite cheongsam, old fashioned mink, / the coral set to match the pink.*

ISBN 962-7160-51-2

New Ends, Old Beginnings
poems by Louise Ho

'Louise Ho's superb new collection of poems ... illuminates and exemplifies many paradoxes, including that strange one that seems to decree that nowadays so much of the sustaining of the Western tradition seems to be done by non-Westerners, and so much reinventing of the culture of the colonisers by the apparently colonised.

'Like another Chinese poet, Mao Tse Tung, she likes to play with images of size, juxtaposing "little" Hong Kong — "this compact commercial enclave" — with "big" China. And amongst the "big" subjects she now tackles are two that are essential for the public poet reflecting upon July 1997 and the like: time and history.'

Michael Hollington
Professor of English at the University of New South Wales, Australia, and the University of Toulon and of Var, France.

ISBN 962-7160-52-0

Egg Woman's Daughter
by Mary Chan

Mary Chan Ma Lai was about two years old when her eyes became inflamed and the corneas clouded over. This was in the early 1950s, and her family was eking out a living fishing the coastal waters of southern China. Her grandmother's treatment with incense ash mixed with mud blinded one eye and blurred the other. That wasn't the last of her afflictions; as Mary grew older spinal infections gradually cost her the use of her legs and she is now confined to a wheelchair.

This book tells the story of Mary's family, their struggle during the times of war and revolution, and Mary's personal victory over her disabilities to become a teacher, writer, world-traveller and vital member of Hong Kong's society.

ISBN 962-7160-53-9

Getting Along With the Chinese
for fun and profit
by Fred Schneiter

The best-selling entertaining and highly informative guide to working and playing with the Chinese.

Schneiter delves into the lighter side of Chinese psychology and demystifies one of the toughest markets in the world. He explains when you should and how you can apply pressure, why patience is not quite the overriding consideration it is generally perceived to be, and what to do and what not to do when hosting Chinese guests.

"An essential item to pack in your 'China survival kit'"
— *The Hongkong Standard*
"Facts on China no degree of study can give"
— *The Shanghai Star*

ISBN 962-7160-19-9

Other titles from Asia 2000

Non-fiction

Cantonese Culture	Shirley Ingram & Rebecca Ng
Concise World Atlas	Maps International
Egg Woman's Daughter	Mary Chan
Getting Along With the Chinese	Fred Schneiter
Hong Kong Pathfinder	Martin Williams
Korean Dynasty — Hyundai and Chung Ju Yung	Donald Kirk
Red Chips and the globalisation of China's enterprises	Charles de Trenck
The Rise & Decline of the Asian Century	Christopher Lingle
Walking to the Mountain	Wendy Teasdill

Fiction

Cheung Chau Dog Fanciers' Society	Alan B Pierce
Chinese Walls	Xu Xi (Sussy Chakó)
Daughters of Hui	Xu Xi (Sussy Chakó)
Getting to Lamma	Jan Alexander
Hong Kong Rose	Xu Xi (Sussy Chakó)
Riding a Tiger	Robert Abel
Temutma	Rebecca Bradley & John Sloan

Poetry

New Ends, Old Beginnings	Louise Ho
Woman to Woman and other poems	Agnes Lam

Order from Asia 2000 Ltd
1101 Seabird House, 22–28 Wyndham St
Central, Hong Kong
tel (852) 2530 1409; fax (852) 2526 1107
email sales@asia2000.com.hk; http://www.asia2000.com.hk/